Fuck Them Kids
A Collection Of Horror Stories
By Timothy King

Savage Rabbit Publishing

Dedication

To my loving wife, Rhianna. Thank you for always supporting me.

To the woman who lives in the walls and the voices in my head, thank you...I guess.

To Jim Groves, Thank you for forcing me to use the title I really wanted

and to the entire Terror Team... you're helping to make my dreams come true.

<u>Trigger Warning</u>

The following stories contain:

Murder

Miscarriage

Domestic Abuse

And overall, rough shit

Read at your own risk!

Foreward

First off, thank you for reading my little (see what I did there?) collection of horrors. This originally started off with a stand-alone short story, Bury Your Demons. I wrote it for fun and had no intention of publishing it. By the time I was done, I felt like it was powerful. I ultimately decided to publish it by itself. After completing that story, the ideas just rolled in and the next thing you know... an anthology was born.

These stories are a compilation of my own fears, both as a consumer of horror and as a father. You will find a variety of stories, all with creepy fucking kids in them. Some are violent, some are subtle, but they're all scary as hell (in my humble opinion).

I am also aware that the title is controversial. I knew it would be when I published it, and I have already received plenty of backlash. At the end of the day, my writing is my art and an expression of self. I love my kids more than anything, but sometimes they can drive me crazy...just like the kids in this collection.

I hope you love these stories as much as I do.

AND

Fuck Them Kids!

Contents

Bury Your Demons

Keith paced back and forth, wearing a short trail into the living room carpet. His hands pressed against the sides of his head, trying to relieve the throbbing tension in his temples. Pain radiated outward from his sore chest and his eyes burned from the copious amount of tears he had shed.

"No. No. No." He muttered as he walked. His head shook subtly back and forth. The tension in his temples seemed to spread at an alarming rate. He began moving his hands erratically around his head, massaging different pressure points, desperate for any relief.

Susan sat completely still on the couch, her face expressionless. Her unkempt blonde hair covered one of her eyes, and a dark red stained her previously white blouse. She sat upright with her ankles crossed and her hands placed delicately on her knees. Her perfect posture sent a ripple of anger coursing through Keith's body. The sheer absurdity of it all infuriated him.

He exploded outward from his well-worn path and grabbed her by the shoulders. Despite his strong grip digging deep into her skin, Susan didn't react. She allowed him to shake her, her head rattling back and forth.

"Why? Why would you do it?" He screamed. Spittle flew from his mouth and coated her face with specks of moisture. "You stupid fucking bitch. How could you?" His face morphed into a deep shade of red. Hatred flared in his eyes. He released her and ran his fingers through his hair. "Oh, God!" In one swift motion, he grabbed the coffee table and flipped it. Magazines and the TV remote flew across the room. Turning back toward his wife he leaned in until his nose was touching hers, summoned a barbaric cry full of anguish, and unleashed it upon her. He continued yelling until there was no more air in his lungs. Weakness flooded his body and he crumpled to his knees in front of her. He lowered his head in defeat. With the last of his strength, he punched the couch. The wood in the armrest gave way and a loud crack filled the air. "How could you?" He cried quietly.

Sensing the fight draining from her husband, Susan reached out slowly, like a child giving a treat to a stranger's dog. When he didn't lash out, she rested her hand on his head. Her fingers weaved themselves through his thick black hair. Keith allowed her to caress him ever so gently, embracing the only good feeling he was experiencing at the moment. More sobs welled up in his throat, threatening to launch him into another inconsolable fit.

"Keith." Susan's voice was entirely void of emotion. "Keith, look at me." She commanded. Slowly, he obeyed, raising his eyes to meet his wife's callous gaze. "You need to pull yourself together. We have to clean this up."

Keith couldn't comprehend what she was saying. His head snapped toward the kitchen, where a pool of blood was slowly carving a path down the tile and soaking into the living room carpet. Little gray toes poked out from around the corner. Images of playing "this little piggie" with his daughter flashed in his mind, causing a wave of physical pain to tear through his body at the realization that he would never play those silly little games with his baby girl again. A weak moan escaped his lips.

"I did what I had to do." She said. "That," she extended one trembling finger toward the kitchen. "Was not our baby girl. That was something else. Something evil."

"You crazy bitch." He muttered.

"Maybe," she replied, "but you're going to help me clean this up. I am your wife, and I did the right thing. Now stand up and go out to the shed." Her bony finger drifted toward the back door. "Dig a hole in the backyard. We have to bury the body." She wrapped her hand around his chin and yanked hard, forcing him to meet her eyes. "Do you understand?"

Reluctantly, he nodded his head and pushed himself to his feet. Shuffling toward the back door, he was careful to avert his eyes from the massacred remains of his baby girl resting in the kitchen. Keith knew that seeing her would destroy him completely. He wouldn't be able to function, let alone dig a hole.

The evening air nipped at the exposed skin on his arms, neck, and head. Goosebumps broke out down his spine. Despite the late hour, the moon illuminated the backyard. He pushed through the discomfort of the chilly night and retrieved the shovel from the shed. Walking across the yard, he embedded the head of the shovel into the ground a few times, searching for a patch of soft dirt. He found one a few feet from the six-foot privacy fence that marked the boundary of his property. Sucking in a deep breath, he plunged the shovel into the ground.

Losing all track of time, he dug away. The muscles in his lower back screamed in agony with every swing of the dirt-filled shovel. The skin of his soft, uncallused hands tore against the rough wood of the shovel's handle. Blood trickled down his arms and dripped into the unconsecrated ground at his feet. He continued digging until he was standing almost shoulder-deep in the earth. Even then, it was only his wife's voice that snapped him out of his trance.

"That's deep enough." She said.

Keith looked around at the enormous hole he had dug, then down at his ruined hands. He tossed the shovel onto the lawn above him and climbed out.

A chill ran through his body at the sight of his wife. She was completely nude. Dried blood coated her body. Her blood-stained clothes sat in a pile at her feet. Without a word, she kicked them into the hole.

Susan stared at Keith expectantly until he relented and pulled off his shirt. He held it loosely in his outstretched hand, allowing it to slide out of his grasp and into the hole. As he slid his pants off, she moved past him and back toward the house. "I'll need your help moving the body." She called back to him.

Burning tears stung his eyes as he tossed his pants into the hole. His legs threatened to give out on him with each shaky step across the yard, until he reached the back door. He leaned against the door frame. Fighting off the imminent panic attack, he sucked in a deep breath and looked into the kitchen.

There, he saw a nude, blood-soaked Susan rolling their little girl into the rug from the dining room. Charlotte's eyes stared at him, void of life. Her slack expression ripped a hole in his soul and seared itself in his memory. He knew at that moment that he would never recover from this. Her tattered throat and soulless eyes would haunt his nightmares forever.

Susan didn't seem to be bothered by it. She simply continued rolling Charlotte up in the rug until the body was completely consumed, and the only thing visible were those cold, gray toes.

"How does that not bother you?" Keith asked incredulously.

Susan stood up, shaking her head. "Because it's not our daughter. It's something else. I knew something was wrong when she started hanging out with that new friend at school." a single tear escaped from the corner of her eye. She quickly wiped it away, smearing blood across her cheek. Shaking her head as if to shake away the emotions, she pointed to the rolled-up carpet. "Pick it up and bury it." She turned to the sink and turned on the water. "I'll finish cleaning up in here."

Reluctantly, Keith stepped forward and grabbed the rug with both hands. He yanked it toward himself. The rough material tore at the cuts and dried blood on his ragged hands. Straining against the dead weight, he managed to wrestle the carpet onto his shoulder. Charlotte never seemed heavy to him before. He recalled throwing her into the air a few days ago, but inside that rug, the seven-year-old's weight was bone-crushing. Keith carefully walked through the back door and continued his labored journey across the yard. Tears poured from his face with every step.

When he reached the hole, he froze. He knew what he had to do but couldn't bring himself to do it. He stood there staring into the darkness at his feet. Thoughts of his daughter being trapped down there ran through his head. He pictured her decaying corpse being devoured by worms and bugs. He must have been standing there for some time because Susan's shrill voice interrupted his morbid thoughts.

"You haven't buried her yet?" She appeared at his side and tossed several blood-soaked towels into the hole. "We don't have long before the sun rises."

"I don't know if I can do it." He whispered. Charlotte's dead weight bore down on his shoulder like the last hug he would ever receive from his daughter.

"Do you want me to go to prison?" She asked, throwing her hands up at her sides. "They won't understand, Keith! They won't believe that she was a monster!"

"That's because she wasn't!" He screamed. "She was our little girl, you fucking bitch." In a fit of anger, he pivoted and released his hold on the body. The bundle collapsed into the hole with a heartbreaking thud. Keith rushed around the hole to retrieve his shovel. He couldn't drag this out; he didn't trust himself to start again if he paused. As quickly as he could, he shoveled. "Is this what you want?" He shouted as he threw heaps of dark soil onto his daughter's body. "You want her gone so fucking bad?" He shouted incoherent sentences and obscenities as he tossed dirt into the hole. Keith worked hard, not stopping for a moment until he had completely filled in the hole, burying his sins.

He tossed the shovel aside and collapsed to the ground, sobbing. Slowly, Susan came to his side and dropped to her knees. She wrapped her arms around him while he cried. The feel of her nude skin on his caused his stomach to churn in revolt. He wanted to run, wanted to call the police, wanted to kill her. But he didn't. He sat there crying for a long time and she held him. They sat huddled like that until the first rays of sunlight broke through the trees at the back of their property.

"We have to shower." She whispered. "We can't let any-one see us like this." Her hands slid off his shoulders. She stood up and held out a hand for him to take.

His eyes drifted back to the loose dirt now covering his little girl, then back to his wife. She reached out and grabbed his hand, coaxing him to his feet. Keith allowed his wife to guide him through the yard and into the house. They paused at the front door so Susan could wash his feet with a wet cloth. She mumbled something about tracking mud into her clean house but Keith wasn't listening anymore. His shattered mind drifted to memories of happier times, his subconscious shielding him from his present reality.

Susan pulled him into the house and pulled the back door closed behind them. She tenderly led him up the stairs and down the hall toward their bedroom. Keith froze as they passed Charlotte's room, yanking his hand away from his wife's. Charlotte's door was cracked open and rays of sunlight leaked through the open window. Susan grabbed the door handle to pull it closed, but out of the corner of his eye, Keith saw the outline of a little girl looking out the window into the backyard. His heart exploded in his chest. He shoved his wife away from the room and smashed into the door with his shoulder. The door crashed into the wall behind it, bouncing back and nearly ripping off his toenail as he entered.

"Charlotte!" He shouted, then froze just inside the door. There was nobody there. His eyes darted wildly around the room, searching desperately for the little girl he had seen."Charlotte?" He pleaded.

Susan's grip on his shoulder caused him to jump.

"She's not in here, Keith." Susan whispered. "Come on." She slid her arm around his shoulders. Susan finished leading Keith down the hallway and into their bathroom. Steam radiated from the walk-in shower. Keith stood submerged in the scalding water, letting it wash away the dirt and shame. His skin turned an angry red from the unrelenting heat. Susan's fingers caressed his arms and back, helping to rid him of the grime. She reached around his body, using her soapy hands to wash his stomach. Her hands drifted lower, teasing at his groin. Her fingers reached his manhood and wrapped around it. He sucked in a deep breath and allowed his head to roll back. He stiffened against her hand as her stroke gained speed. For a few seconds all of the bad in his life washed away. He was about to lose himself to the excitement when the image of his dead daughter flashed in his mind. Everything came flooding back and he slapped her hand away.

"What're you doing?" He snapped.

She rested her cheek against his shoulder. "Just trying to take your mind off everything." She whispered.

Another surge of rage flooded through his body. Keith slowly turned around to face his wife, stifling the urge to smash her head into the bathroom tiles. Her emotionless eyes stared back at him, making it that much harder to restrain himself. "I really need to understand." He said.

Susan lowered her eyes. "You know why." She said firmly. "That wasn't our little girl anymore. I don't know how many times I have to say it." She reached past Keith and turned off the water. Stepping out of the shower, she grabbed a towel and dried her hair. Without looking at Keith, she added, "I did the right thing." She quickly wrapped the towel around herself and disappeared into their bedroom.

Keith stepped out of the shower, his hands shaking uncontrollably. Nausea broiled in his stomach. He tried to fight it back, but the acid liquid burned the back of his throat. He tossed open the toilet bowl and vomited into it. He threw up two more times before the nausea subsided. The muscles in his lower back cramped painfully and he slumped to the ground next to the toilet. Not bothering to get up, he reached around blindly on the counter and pulled down his towel before quickly drying himself off. Using the toilet for support, he hoisted himself to his feet and staggered out of the bathroom.

Susan was already in her spot on the right side of the bed, facing away from him. Her nude shoulders rose and fell rhythmically with her breathing. He clenched his fists. A bolt of anger tore through him. How could she do it? He knew Charlotte had been acting strange lately, but that was no excuse. If anything, the poor girl was sick. Instead of getting her help, the one person who was supposed to protect her tore her throat out in a vicious fashion. He wanted to wrap his tattered hands around Susan's neck and squeeze the life from her. He wanted to see the look in her eyes as the realization that she was dying set in. The image of his daughter's eyes staring at him as his wife rolled her body into the rug flashed in his mind and he wondered if his wife would have the same, cold look.

Keith inhaled deeply and unclasped his fists. The exhaustion was wearing him down, and he couldn't think straight. He shook the images from his mind, breathing slowly a few more times to compose himself. Giving into the drowsiness, he collapsed onto his side of the bed and drifted off to sleep.

"This little piggy went to market."

Keith awoke with a start when someone yanked on his big toe. He tried to sit up but some unseen force pressed him firmly into the bed. The midday sun streaming through their bedroom windows burned his retinas, forcing him to squint his eyes against the blinding light.

"This little piggy stayed home."

Icy fingers squeezed the next toe tightly. Keith's blood ran cold. The voice was hollow and monotone, a mockery of a little girl's voice. He forced his eyes open and couldn't believe what he saw.

Standing at the foot of his bed was Charlotte. Thick clumps of mud clung to her hair. The gashes in her throat seeped blood that ran down her chest in grotesque rivers. It coagulated into a disgusting soup at her feet.

"Charlotte?" He croaked.

"This little piggy had roast beef." Her fingers drifted to the third toe on his right foot. His eyes darted to the side to see his wife sleeping with her back to him.

Keith tried to sit up again, but that same invisible weight pinned him to the bed.

"This little piggy had none." The hollow, lifeless voice of his daughter rang out.

"Charlotte, baby, I'm so sorry." Tears carved a path through the stubble on his face. "I should've done more to help you. I should've stopped her."

A smile stretched across Charlotte's face. The sickly gray tint of her skin caused Keith's stomach to lurch, but he kept his eyes trained on his little girl.

"This little piggy went wee, wee, wee all the way home." With unnatural speed and precision, her hand darted out and gripped the pinky toe on his right foot and twisted. Agonizing pain tore through Keith's leg. He screamed and thrashed against his invisible restraints. His eyes clenched shut involuntarily as the warm sensation of his own blood spurted from the wound. When he looked back at Charlotte, she held his pinky toe between two fingers for him to see. She wiggled it back and forth.

"Susan!" Keith shrieked. "Susan, wake up!"

Charlotte laughed. "Susan!" She mimicked his voice nearly perfectly. "Susan, wake up!" She giggled. Charlotte's corpse launched the severed toe at her father. It smacked against Keith's cheek with a meaty thud. His chest rose and fell in rapid succession.

"My cunt of a mother won't wake up." Charlotte crept around the side of the bed until she was next to Susan. Slowly, she reached out and pushed on the woman's shoulder.

Susan's head lulled to the side, her eyes stretched open in terror. Keith's eyes drifted down to her neck and his mouth gaped wide. He tried to scream, but only a squeak came out. His wife's neck was torn open, revealing jagged chunks of white bone. The lacerations were deep enough to nearly decapitate her. Susan's head hung on by a few patches of stringy skin.

Keith thrashed against invisible restraints, fighting with every fiber of his being to reach out to his apparently dead wife.

Standing next to Susan's nearly headless body, Charlotte laughed. Her laughter grew harder and harder with every second until the monstrosity hunched over, gasping for air.

"What's so fucking funny?" Keith shouted.

Charlotte stopped laughing. She lifted her head and smiled at her father. One of her cold hands snapped out and grabbed Susan's shoulder. With one tug, she rolled the corpse onto the floor. Hopping over Susan, the Charlotte creature climbed into the bed. Her hair fell wildly around her face. It tickled Keith's nose as she leaned in close. Charlotte pressed her lips to her father's ears.

"Mommy was right." Keith willed himself to move but could not even lift a finger. Charlotte grabbed onto the wall behind the headboard and sunk her fingers into the drywall. She hoisted herself up, climbing the wall like a spider until she dangled from the roof. Her head snapped backward, a sickening crunch reverberating through the room. Muddy clumps of blood and tissue fell from the open wound in her neck, covering him in gore. "I'm not your little girl." The creature that looked like Charlotte smiled. "I ripped her to pieces in the woods."

"No! I'll fucking kill you!" He shouted. Spittle flew from his lips. The muscles in his neck strained, the veins bulging under his skin. "I'll fucking kill you!"

The Charlotte creature dropped back onto the bed with a thud. It stepped over Keith's stomach and straddled him.

In a perfect imitation of his daughter, the creature cried. Tears poured down its face. "You already did that, Daddy. Don't you remember?" She lowered her head, and her long, mud-caked hair obscured her face. "You buried me." The voice mockery slipped away with the word 'me', and the undead creature's own baritone reverberated off the walls of the room.

"Why are you doing this?" He shouted.

It snapped its head back up. "Because I can." It whispered. The Charlotte thing walked two fingers up Keith's chest. They stopped at the soft patch of flesh between the collarbones. Charlotte's warped and horrific visage leaned in close, their noses nearly touching. The decaying stench of his daughter's corpse permeated Keith's nostrils. Slowly, the Charlotte demon applied pressure to the tender flesh at the base of his neck. It was uncomfortable at first, then morphed into agony as the fingers broke through the flesh. Heat rushed around his neck and shoulders as blood seeped from the open wound.

Keith screamed out in pain, but the approaching sound of a police siren drowned out his cries. Charlotte's head snapped in the direction of the bedroom door.

"Looks like playtime is over." The creature hissed. It rolled off the bed, collapsing to the floor with a thud.

Keith sucked in a deep breath. He sat up in bed, finally able to move freely. Throwing the covers aside, he exposed his nude, blood-soaked body to the cold night air.

Keith hurled himself off the bed and to his wife's side. Hot tears poured from his eyes, and snot bubbled from his nose. He allowed himself to collapse against the wall and was resting his head in his hands when something bright caught his eyes.

Reaching under the bed to retrieve the object, he quickly realized it was Susan's cell phone. Turning it over, he saw it was open to a text thread with Susan's mother. The last text from Susan read, "Send help. Keith killed Charlotte."

Keith's blood froze in his body. Nausea rumbled and threatened to spew over. The sirens were in his front yard now, creating an ear-shattering howl. The sound of the front door to the house exploding open rang out. A series of voices started shouting from downstairs. He could make out phrases like "sheriff's office" and "show yourself."

The phone slipped from his hand and shattered against the tile floor. Susan's blood coated the phone, seeping into the cracks until the screen went out. Keith slipped into a state of delirium. A laugh crept up his throat. It started as a smirk, then a light chuckle. Finally, it grew to a ridiculous bellowing cackle.

A few seconds later, the door to his bedroom burst open and three cops piled into the room, pistols drawn. There was a series of incomprehensible shouts coming from the officers. Keith locked eyes with Charlotte's deceased corpse.

A smirk wormed its way onto her face as an officer slammed Keith's face down into the tile. The smirk grew bigger when the officer ruthlessly snapped the handcuffs into place.

Just as the officers prepared to drag him from the room, Charlotte winked.

In The House Of The Devil

Father William Jones opened the door of his car and stepped out. The crisp fall air of northern Ohio rushed to meet him, carrying red and brown leaves down the street. He pulled his coat closed and buried his hands in his pockets.

Behind him, the passenger door of the church's black sedan slammed shut, rocking the vehicle. Father Jones rolled his eyes at his young passenger's eagerness. Gently closing his own door with his elbow, he spoke to the other man without looking at him. "Keilan, get my bags." He walked across the street without waiting for the other man to answer him.

He approached a house that sat on a modest parcel of land, surrounded by a chain link fence. A single-car driveway rose up to a detached garage with broken gutters that hung uselessly from the roof. Paint peeled from the walls and a moldy plank of plywood covered a broken window. The building sat juxtaposed with the surrounding neighborhood. Looking up and down the street, Father Jones saw well-manicured lawns and freshly painted houses.

Father Jones exhaled and shook his head. Glancing down at his watch, he waited for the hand to tick to five, then entered the gate, leaving it open for Keilan. His dress shoes clicked across the concrete walkway and clattered loudly when he climbed the front steps of the house. He raised his fist to knock, but the door flew open before he could.

"Father Jones?" A middle-aged woman asked. Her brown hair was pulled into a messy bun at the top of her head. He could tell she tried to cover up her grays with hair dyeing kits, but it was no use. They stuck out like scratches on a nice car. Deep blue bags lined her eyes, making her appear much older than she was. She stared expectantly at the priest, desperation chalked across her face.

"Yes." Father Jones said flatly. He removed his right hand and held it out for the woman to shake.

The woman reached out and gripped his hand between both of hers. "Bless you, Father." She whispered. Her hands lingered there while tears built up in the corners of her eyes and threatened to fall. "Thank you so much for coming." She whispered.

The two lingered there for a moment longer. Feeling the awkwardness between them, Father Jones broke the silence. "May I come in?"

The woman's eyes stretched wide. She pulled her hand away and stepped aside, holding the door for the priest. "Of course." She nearly shouted. Waving a hand to beckon the priest forward, she mumbled an apology.

Father Jones stepped through the doorway, nodding his thanks to the woman as he passed. His lips turned up into a grimace at the sight of the house. It was far worse than the exterior. Dirty dishes lined the coffee and dining room tables. A pile of soiled tissues stretched upward like the Tower of Babel on the couch. An old tube TV rested directly on the yellowed carpet. A black and white show silently played on, casting light and shadows around the room.

This wasn't the first time Father Jones had been in a house like this, and with the new Bishop, it was becoming an all too common occurrence. In fact, he was pretty sure Bishop Anderson had made it his life's mission to find the most disgusting places to send him to. He subtly shook his head. The old Bishop was determined to have a "real" exorcism performed within his diocese.

The woman shuffled past a pile of trash and made her way to the couch. She quickly scooped up the tissues and carried them to the kitchen, disappearing from sight around a wall separating the two rooms. When she returned, she wore a mortified expression, her pale complexion now bright red. She glanced around the room before motioning to the couch. "I apologize for the mess, Father. I haven't had much of a chance to clean." She lowered her head and dropped her voice to a whisper. "I've been too busy taking care of my daughter." She motioned with her head to a hallway at the back of the house. "She has become..." Her words drifted off. Shaking her head, she said, " Well, I guess you will see shortly." She forced a smile, trying to make herself seem more friendly and inviting.

Father Jones nodded and moved around the coffee table. He reluctantly dropped himself onto the couch, careful not to let his sleeve touch what looked like a glob of ketchup.

"I'm Helen." The woman said, realizing she never introduced herself. "Helen Jackson."

Father Jones nodded. "It's a pleasure to meet you, Mrs. Jackson."

Helen smiled at the priest. Her eyes quickly darted to the front door as Keilan made his way in, carrying a large box of supplies. The young man's forehead was dotted with sweat, despite the cold. He stumbled through the doorway, his frail frame struggling to hold the box any longer.

"Excuse my intrusion." He said through gritted teeth. "But do you have somewhere I could set this?"

Helen rushed to the coffee table. She quickly stacked the various dishes precariously on top of each other. Lifting them up, she balanced them with the skill of a circus performer and motioned with her head. "You can set it right there." For the second time in as many minutes, Helen disappeared into the kitchen.

The morbid thought crossed Father Jones' mind that if they stayed long enough, this woman might clean her whole house. He had to stifle a laugh.

Keilan looked at the priest for approval. He gasped with relief when Father Jones nodded. The skinny man nearly dropped the box. It crashed onto the coffee table with a thud.

"Careful with that, you fool." Father Jones hissed.

Keilan recoiled at the scolding and lowered his head. "Sorry, Father."

Father Jones shook his head. "It's fine. Just be careful." He examined the young man with disdain in his eyes.

Keilan opened his mouth to reply but closed it when Helen entered the room. She was wiping her hands on a dish rag she then tossed on the dining room table. "So."

She said, placing her hands on her hips. "Should I take you to see her?"

Father Jones held out his hand in a stopping motion. "We will see the girl, but first, I have some questions." He rubbed his chin as he spoke. "Also, I would like to explain the process to you. It's not exactly..." he trailed off, glancing at the TV in the corner of the room. "Like you see in the movies."

"Of course, Father. Whatever you need."

Father Jones held out a hand toward Keilan, who produced a leather-bound notebook and pen from the supplies box.

Double-clicking the pen, Father Jones drew a few lines to test the ink. Satisfied, he looked back up to Helen.

"I have most of this information in my files." He used the pen to point at the box. "But I always like to get my information directly from the source. What is your daughter's name?"

"Rebecca Howard."

Father Jones jotted down some notes.

"Her father passed away and I remarried. That's why she has a different last name." Helen quickly added. "It's not like she was born out of wedlock or anything."

Father Jones nodded, seemingly uninterested in Helen's attempt to rationalize the trivial information.

"And you believe your daughter is possessed by a demon." He said it flatly, no hint of a question in his voice. Tearing his eyes away from his paper, he raised his gaze to meet Helen's, the two of them locking eyes. "Why?"

She wiped the tears from her cheeks. "She's always been a good girl, but a couple of months ago, she got caught smoking in the bathroom at school."

Father Jones scribbled in his notebook without taking his eyes off Helen. "Cigarettes or Marijuana?" The priest asked.

Helen covered her eyes with her right hand. "Both, I'm afraid. That's how it started. Drinking and drugs. Then it was the…" Helen looked like she was agonizing over the words. They caught in her throat and she fought to get them out. "Promiscuity." She blurted. "Just a parade of boys. One after another, no matter what I did or said." Her cheeks flushed again. "Then it was the blasphemy." Helen took a short step back and leaned against the wall. "That's when I got suspicious."

"And when did you know for sure?" Father Jones asked.

Terror stretched across Helen's face. She sank lower against the wall, sliding down until her butt hit the ground. Her shoulders sagged. She whispered something unintelligible and crossed herself.

"I'm sorry, I couldn't hear you." Father Jones said.

Her head snapped up, and all the color drained from her face. "The stigmata." She whispered. The dam finally broke, and the tears fell freely now. Within seconds, several months' worth of grief and stress overwhelmed her and she devolved into hysterical sobs.

Keilan quickly crossed himself and cupped his hand in front of his chest. He lowered his head and uttered a quick prayer.

Father Jones closed his book and set it on the table. He tossed the pen into the box and looked at Keilan. "I think it's time I meet Rebecca." Keilan reached into the box and pulled out a folded piece of white fabric. His hands trembled as he held it out to Father Jones, who then removed his coat, carefully folding it and setting it onto the armrest, narrowly missing the ketchup stain. Just as he had done countless times before, Father Jones slid the surplice over his clothes. He held out his hand toward Keilan, "my stole?" Keilan quickly dug out the purple stole and handed it to the priest.

Father Jones brought the stole to his lips. Closing his eyes, he said a quick prayer and kissed the cloth before draping it over his shoulders.

Helen moved to stand up, but Father Jones held out a hand. "I'll talk to her alone. I need to judge the validity of this alleged possession myself." Helen opened her mouth to protest, but Father Jones beat her to it. "This is the way it has to be." He said. Turning back to his assistant, he pointed at the box. "Unpack the crosses, holy water, and my Bible. Be prepared to bring them into the room should I require them."

"Yes, Father." Keilan said.

Father Jones turned his attention back to Helen. "I'm not sure how long I'll be in there, but I will call for you if we need anything." Shifting his weight off his bad foot, he hobbled toward the hallway.

The hallway was long and poorly lit. Like the rest of the house, it was littered with trash and dirty dishes. They were cluttered against the wall, allowing only a narrow walkway down the center. The air vent on the wall was black with dirt and dust, nearly blending the vent in with the wall. A lone crucifix depicting Jesus on the cross adorned the otherwise bare walls.

Father Jones reached into his pocket and withdrew his own crucifix. Quickly crossing himself, he continued toward the furthest bedroom. As he approached, the air grew warmer. A single bead of sweat rolled down his back. The repugnant malodor of shit grew stronger. It wafted from the bedroom, filling the stale air around him. Fighting back a gag, he pushed himself forward. The stench grew stronger and Father Jones imagined himself walking into the room to see a dead girl on the floor.

Father Jones was accustomed to death. He had conducted more last rites than he cared to remember. Once, he had even attended an exorcism that went wrong, resulting in a young girl's death. The life draining from a person's eyes always pained him, and he hoped he wouldn't see it again on this day.

The door to the bedroom screamed teenage girl. A sign that read, "Knock first" hung above pictures of various rockstars and bands that Father Jones didn't recognize.

He crossed himself again and whispered, "Lord give me strength." Raising his hand, he allowed his fist to linger inches from the door. Closing his eyes, he knocked.

"Come in!" An innocent sounding voice said from within the room.

Father Jones grabbed the handle and paused. He took a second to consider the optics of himself being alone with a teenage girl in her room, then shook it off. The two needed to be able to speak freely in order for him to assess the need for an exorcism properly.

Father Jones entered the room, expecting to find more of the same teenage girlishness he had seen on the door. Instead, he balked at the scene, slowly taking in all of its horrors. The gruesome details rose up to meet him, over-whelming his senses.

The pink walls were covered with flies. They buzzed about obnoxiously, landing at will across the walls. Holes pockmarked the drywall, making it look as if a boxer had gone ten rounds with the wall. Dirty dishes covered a desk, crusty mold affixing them to the surface. The Priest's eyes drifted from horror to horror, growing worse as he took it all in. In the corner of the room sat a bucket, filled to the brim with a brown mud-like substance. The stench wafting from it told him it was human feces. He gagged and turned away from it.

That's when his eyes finally fell on Rebecca.

She was splayed out on her bed, lying on her back. Her eyes rotated in their sockets, seemingly keeping pace with the ceiling fan. Brown hair hung in matted clumps from her greasy head. Her sallow cheeks appeared gaunt and expressionless. A large white comforter, stained yellow, covered her to her chin.

Father Jones swallowed hard and took a step forward. "Good Evening, Rebecca. I'm Father Jones.

Rebecca slowly turned her head toward the priest. She stared at him blankly for a moment, then, as if recognizing someone she knew, her eyes brightened. Tears flowed freely down those emaciated cheeks.

"Oh, thank you, God." She whispered. Locking eyes with the priest, she smiled. "He has delivered me." Her eyes flicked back to the door. "You have to help me." She whispered.

Father Jones nodded. "I intend to do just that." He pointed at the chair by the computer desk. "Do you mind if I sit?"

The girl shook her head. She watched while the priest moved the chair closer to the bed and brushed off the seat. The chair moaned in protest against the priest's weight.

Father Jones chuckled. "I guess I need to lay off Sister Mary's cookies."

Rebecca didn't respond. Her face had returned to the absent appearance it had when the priest had entered the room.

Leaning forward in the chair, Father Jones placed his elbows on his knees, doing his best to bring himself to her level. "So, I hear you haven't been feeling well." He said.

Rebecca shook her head. "I was fine." She paused, allowing the tears to run down her face and absorb into her pillow. "It's my mom that's sick." She whispered.

Father Jones looked around the room and nodded. "How so?" He encouraged her.

"You see the house, don't you?" She snapped. "It wasn't always like this." Rebecca choked back a sob. She sucked in a long, deep breath to compose herself. "This all started a couple weeks ago, when my stepdad left."

Father Jones sighed. He had seen this several times before. Religious people in crisis tended to attribute their problems to external factors... such as demons. Images of so many alleged exorcisms passed through his mind in an instant.

"So you're saying your mother is sick?" He asked tentatively.

She nodded slowly. Her lips trembled. "Pull down the covers." She insisted.

Father Jones reached out, his hand lingering for a moment between them. A part of him suspected this was nothing but the musing of a sick woman, but another part of him knew he was being deceived. The question he had to answer was *by whom?*

He gripped the top of the comforter. Crusty residue cracked under his grip, coating his hand in dried bodily fluids. Slowly, he pulled the comforter back.

At first, nothing seemed out of the ordinary. The teenager was in a once pink nightgown, now dingy gray with sweat and dirt. He pulled the covers down further, averting his eyes as the comforter passed over the mounds of her breasts. He slid the comforter a little further, then froze. Draped across the girl's midsection was a thick black strap, velcroed into place.

He stared at the strap in disbelief as his mouth fell open.

"There's more." Rebecca whispered with tears in her eyes.

Father Jones pulled the comforter back further to reveal two more black straps fastened around the girl's forearms. The skin around the Velcro had blistered into an angry shade of red. He couldn't help but wince at the obviously painful sight. His eyes tracked further down her arm to her hands.

Father Jones dropped to his knees next to the girl's bed and crossed himself. Squeezing his eyes shut, he frantically uttered a prayer.

"Father." Rebecca interrupted. When Father Jones continued praying, Rebecca leaned as far as the straps would allow her. "Father." She said forcefully.

Father Jones' eyes snapped open.

"It's not a miracle." Rebecca glanced down at the holes in her hands. The festering wound oozed a greenish pus from the opening. Looking down, she could see directly through her palm to the white sheets of her bed. "My mother did this to me." She whispered. Her eyes pleaded with him to help.

"Your mother?" He asked.

"Yes, Father." Her chest rose and fell in rapid succession. She allowed herself to slump back against her pillow. "She drove stakes through my hands to make it look like I carried the stigmata." Looking away from the priest, she stared at the wall. "My mother is sick." She whispered.

Father Jones slowly extended his arm and rested it on Rebecca's shoulder. "Don't worry, my child." He patted her shoulder and stood up. "We will get you help.

"Thank you." Rebecca whispered.

Father Jones walked across the room and grabbed the door handle.

"Oh, and Father?" Rebecca stopped him. "Don't listen to her. She's a master manipulator."

Father Jones nodded and exited the room. He power-walked down the hall and into the living room.

Helen was sitting on the couch next to Keilan. Keilan was dutifully jotting down notes in the notebook, the artifacts of exorcism arrayed neatly on the coffee table.

Father Jones reached out and took Helen's hand in his own, interrupting Keilan's interview. "Helen, I need you to tell me the truth. How did your daughter get the stigmata?" Father Jones stared deep into Helen's eyes, desperate to find the truth.

Helen looked away. "I-I don't know, Father." She stammered. "She was out with some friends at the park, the next thing I know, she's screaming in the bathroom. Her hands were under the facet, and there was blood everywhere." Helen returned her gaze to the priest.

Father Jones stared at her a little longer, then turned his gaze upon Keilan. "The girl is strapped to her bed." Keilan's face shifted in surprise. The two had done several exorcisms together and never once had they tied down the afflicted person. "Go untie her." He ordered.

Keilan snapped his notebook closed and tossed it into the box he had carried in. Pushing himself off the couch, he marched past the others and directly to Rebecca's room.

"No, Father. Please. She's dangerous." Helen shifted uncomfortably in her seat. She stole frantic glances over her shoulder, watching as Keilan disappeared from view. "She might hurt him." she pleaded.

Kneeling to her level, Father Jones took her other hand, "Every day I meet people who think their family member is possessed. Do you know how many are true cases of possession?" He tilted his head, beckoning her to try and answer the question.

"How many?" She asked.

"Almost none." He said confidently. The sound of velcro being unstrapped filled the room. "Most," he made air quotes with his fingers, "possessions," he returned his hand to hers. "They're simply mental illnesses." Shrugging, he continued. "I think that's what's happening here, and we're going to help you."

He opened his mouth to speak again but was cut off by a massive thud, followed by a scream coming from the bedroom. Father Jones leaned against the couch, using it to lift himself up. Helen pushed past him, sprinting down the hallway toward Rebecca's room. Father Jones followed her, the pair reaching the door at nearly the same time.

Keilan screamed again. The young man was flat on his back with his hands up, protecting his face. Above him, Rebecca raised a thick textbook and brought it down again. It smashed into Keilan's arms, not doing much damage, but the man yelped in pain. Rebecca tossed the book aside. She threw her head back and shrieked at the ceiling, the veins in her neck protruding.

Helen reacted first, rushing into the room and grabbing her daughter around the waist. The woman dug her feet into the floor, fighting with every ounce of her strength to drive her daughter toward the bed. After a few steps, Rebecca laughed.

It wasn't the laugh of a teenage girl hanging out with her friends.

It was deeper. Sinister.

Father Jones' blood ran cold. He'd heard a laugh like that three times before. It was a laugh he had hoped to never hear again. It was the laugh of a demon.

The guttural laugh boomed out of the beautiful young girl's mouth, echoing off the walls. With a swift motion, she grabbed her mother's throat and began to squeeze. The muscles in her arm flexed, bulging impossibly large as she twisted, apparently trying to snap the woman's neck.

"Father Jones!" Keilan shouted.

The sound of his name spurred him forward. He withdrew the crucifix from his pocket and held it out in front of him.

"In the name of Jesus Christ, I order you to drop that woman!" He shouted.

There was a moment when nobody moved. The four stood locked in a battle of wills. Rebecca squeezed a little tighter, then let go. Helen slumped to the ground at Rebecca's feet. Her hands flew to her throat as her body heaved with violent coughs. The purple tint of her face started to subside and after a moment, she crawled backward toward the priest.

"What's the matter, mother? Cat got your tongue?" Rebecca mocked. She put her hands to her throat, blood seeping from the open wounds in her palms and pretended to cough. Spit flew from her mouth with each pretend cough.

Holding the cross out, Father Jones took a step toward Rebecca. "I command you to return to the bed."

Rebecca cocked her head toward the priest. "And I demand that you suck my dick." She snapped. Giggling, she took a step toward Keilan. "Actually, he probably would." She hissed, pointing at Keilan.

Father Jones jumped into action, positioning himself between the girl and his assistant. "In the name of God, I command you to return to the bed."

Rebecca's eyes stretched open wide. Her injured hands flew to her mouth and she gasped. "What is happening?" She asked, her voice returning to normal. Her chest quivered and tears streamed from her face. "What did I do?" She asked. Her face flew from Father Jones to Keilan before landing on her injured mother.

Father Jones took a cautious step forward. "It's ok, Rebecca. I'm going to help you. Can you please get back in the bed?" He asked.

The scared look on Rebecca's face disappeared in an instant, replaced by a smile. She uncovered her mouth and nibbled on the tip of her finger. With her other hand, she twirled her brown hair. "You want me to get in the bed,

Father?" A girlish giggle escaped her lips. "Why? Are you going to strap me down again?"

Father Jones tightened his grip on the cross. "Only so we can help you. Now, please." He motioned toward the bed with his free hand. "Get into bed."

"So you can fuck me?" She asked sharply. Every hint of girlish flirting had drained from her voice. She locked eyes on the priest, who was already shaking his head. "Why not?" She raised both hands, showing the priest the holes in her palms. "I even have extra holes!" Her voice rang out, echoing unnaturally.

"Rebecca, please!" Helen shouted.

Father Jones took a step toward the girl, the cross extended to lead the way. "Helen, check on Keilan." He ordered.

"I'm fine." Keilan snapped, climbing to his feet. Blood dripped from deep scratches in his cheek and a dark blue lump was growing on his forehead. "I shouldn't have let her get the jump on me."

Rebecca's infected hands slid down the front of her nightdress, stopping just above her crotch. "You can..." She trailed off, running her hands back up her body and into her hair. Her hands left a trail of pus across the front of her nightgown. She bit her lip and locked eyes with Keilan. "Jump me." She finished.

Keilan took a faltering step backward. The young man closed his eyes and bowed his head. "Our Father, who art in Heaven." He whispered.

Rebecca turned away from the men and jumped onto her bed. "You guys are no fun!" She screamed. Looking around as if confused, she rocked up and down. Convinced the bed was sturdy enough, Rebecca jumped. Her feet barely left the mattress, but she giggled playfully, bouncing again. Her nightgown flared with each bounce, showing more and more of her upper thighs. She stopped jumping and snapped her head toward Father Jones.

"I saw you looking, pervert." She hissed.

"Demon! I commanded you in the name of Holy God to lie down on this bed!" Father Jones yelled, ignoring the quip. He took another step forward. "Keilan, my Bible." Stretching out his free hand, he waited for Keilan to hand it over.

"It's not going to work." Rebecca chided in a sing-song voice. She patted down her nightgown, then dropped to the bed, sitting criss crossed at the center. "Seriously, it's not going to work." Locking eyes with Keilan, she placed her hand on her thigh. Using one finger to trace across her skin, she inched her night gown up, revealing her white panties. "Last chance, Keilan." She whispered. Giving him a wink, she let the gown fall back into place.

Father Jones flipped through his Bible, opening it to Psalm 53. "God, by your name save me."

Rebecca rolled her eyes. "God, by your name save me." She mocked in a high-pitched voice. "Seriously? This old song and dance?" She scooted to the edge of the bed, allowing her feet to dangle off. "And by your might defend my cause." She finished.

Ignoring her, Father Jones read the next line. "And by your might defend my cause."

Rebecca rolled her eyes. "I'm getting bored, priest." She pushed herself up, standing directly in front of Father Jones. "Let's skip to the good part." She winked. Twirling in a circle, she outstretched her arms, mimicking Jesus on the cross. "My name is Asmodeus!" The demon's voice rang out incredibly loud, declaring itself to the world. It stopped spinning and locked eyes with Father Jones. "And I am the demon of lust." It whispered.

Father Jones' eyes flicked down toward the Bible. He tried to read off the next line in the Psalm, but his throat felt tight. The clerical collar around his neck tightened. Dropping his Bible, his hands went to his neck. The collar contracted while he struggled to slide his finger between it and his neck.

"Father?" Keilan asked. "Father, what's wrong?" The young man rushed across the room to Father Jones' side.

Father Jones leaned back, pointing frantically at his collar. His face morphed from tan to purple, getting darker with every passing second. Keilan grabbed the collar and pulled, nearly yanking Father Jones off his feet. The priest collapsed to his knees. Spittle flew from his mouth and his eyes bulged.

Keilan watched helplessly as the blood vessels in his mentor's eyes burst, staining the white parts a bright red. Blood spurted from Father Jones' nose, coating Keilan's pants.

"I can't get it off!" Keilan screamed. He yanked harder on the collar. Despite his best efforts, it continued tightening until an ear-shattering *crack* filled the room.

Father Jones slumped forward and collapsed face down on the ground.

Somewhere behind Keilan, Helen screamed. He heard the patter of her feet down the hall and the sound of her talking in the kitchen. Every fiber of his being told him to run. If he made it out the front door he could scream for help or just keep running until he collapsed. Looking up from Father Jones' lifeless body, he locked eyes with the demon in Rebecca's body and knew he would never leave this room of his own free will.

Rebecca cracked her neck and sat back on the bed. "What's the matter Keilan?" She asked innocently. Her eyes drifted down to the dead priest then back up to Keilan. "Oops." She giggled. "He was so boring." She threw her hands up and let them fall to her side. "He wanted to sit there and read Bible verses. I've read them all and you know what?"

Keilan weighed his options. The little training he had told him not to engage with the demon, but his gut told him differently. If he kept her entertained, she might not kill him right away. Slowly shaking his head, he asked, "What?"

An enormous grin stretched across Rebecca's face. She clapped her hands and laughed, rocking back and forth in the bed. "It's full of shit!"

Keilan shook his head. "Not all of it." He protested. "Demons are real."

Rebecca quit laughing but her smile never faded. She pointed a finger at him and wagged it a couple of times. "I knew you were the smart one." She hissed. Then she shrugged, "So what do you want to do?" The demon asked.

"Wh-what do I want to do?" He stuttered.

"Yeah. We have a couple minutes to kill before the police show up. You could pick up the Bible again and try to exorcise me?"

Keilan looked down. The corner of the Bible stuck out from underneath Father Jones. He started to reach for it but stopped when Rebecca spoke again.

"But I wouldn't." She said quickly. "Because then I'd have to kill you." Her words were menacing, but her tone was playful, almost as if she were flirting with him. She leaned back on the bed, forcing her chest outward to draw focus to her breasts. "We could do other things." Her eyes looked him up and down, drinking him in.

"I can't imagine you rose up from Hell to seduce me." Keilan quipped.

The demon smiled. "I came to seduce the world." Her hands danced along the inside of her thighs as she thrust her hips up and down. Before Keilan could react, Rebecca slammed her hands into the bed, pushing herself to her feet. In the blink of an eye, she closed the distance between them. Her hands wrapped around his head and pulled him close to her. She pressed her lips to his ear. "The police are coming." Rebecca nibbled on his earlobe. "They all wear cameras now." Her head swung back and whipped around to the other side of his head, where she licked sweat from his neck. "The whole world will finally see."

Keilan shook, holding as still as he could. In his mind, he prayed for God to spare him. He begged for the Lord to cast this demon back to Hell. He prayed for God to do anything in that moment.

Rebecca slid her tongue up to his cheek. As if reading his mind, the torment continued. "God has abandoned humanity." She said confidently.

Keilan didn't want to believe it, but something inside of him broke. It felt like someone reminding him of a word he'd forgotten or meeting up with a long lost friend. She was telling the truth and somewhere deep inside, He had known it for some time.

From outside, the sound of sirens filled the air. They heard the screech of tires and shouting voices.

"Time to go." The demon said. She grabbed Keilan's shoulder and spun him around. With incredible strength she drove him forward, pushing him down the hallway. They rounded the corner and could see her mother in the kitchen, crying into her cell phone. "Stop." The demon commanded.

Keilan still held on to the tiniest sliver of hope that he would find a way out of this. Not wanting to push the demon any further, he did as he was told.

Rebecca released his shoulder and entered the kitchen. She stood over her sobbing mother for a moment, then turned and strutted to the counter. A block of knives sat on the counter and Rebecca slid one out. The blade made a cutting sound as she pulled it across the sharpener. Turning back to her mother, knife in hand, she marched across the room.

"Do you know why Rebecca played with the Ouija board that day?" Asmodeus asked.

Helen shook her head.

"To get away from your husband." With every syllable, Rebecca's sweet voice faded, replaced with the sinister baritone of the demon. It ran one of its ruined hands through its hair, pulling away loose clumps. Leaning in close, it whispered just loud enough for Keilan to hear. "He touched her every night." Without hesitation, it plunged the knife deep into Helen's chest. She rocked back and grabbed Rebecca's arm. Her hands pulled frantically at Rebecca's. Blood seeped from her lips. The demon pulled away so it could lock eyes with Helen. It watched as the life faded from her eyes while a smile danced on its face.

The demon spun on its heels, wiping its bloodied hands on Rebecca's night down. Red handprints stained the front, mixing with the weeks of sweat and piss that had built up. She rushed across the kitchen, snatching Keilan by the arm. Her fingers dug deep into his skin, causing him to wince.

"If you do as I say, you might make it out of this." Asmodeus said in its hauntingly deep voice.

Keilan nodded, unable to form a coherent sentence. He allowed the demon to push him toward the front door.

"This is the police!" A man's voice shouted from outside the house. "Come outside with your hands where we can see them!" Keilan heard more tires screeching to a stop outside the house, followed by the opening and closing of doors. He glanced back at the demon.

She was smiling.

"It's show time." The demon said. It bounced up and down on its toes, clenching and unclenching its fists. "I'm kind of nervous. You ever get nervous about public speaking?" The demon asked.

Keilan slowly turned his head to face the demon.

Rebecca's beautiful smile peered back at him. She still looked so much like a normal teenager, if you could look past the blood.

"Let's do this." Asmodeus said, projecting his voice to sound like Rebecca's again. It reached forward and grabbed the handle. Taking a deep breath, it flung the door open.

Cold air rushed into the room, blowing leaves into the walkway. Keilan raised a hand, shielding his eyes from the sudden change in lighting.

"Get down on the ground right now!" A deep voice boomed.

Keilan dropped his hand to see three police officers standing at the end of the driveway, pistols drawn. As Keilan's eyes tunneled in on the barrels of the guns, he lost sight of the details of the officers. Rebecca placed a hand on his shoulder and shoved him toward the police. Keilan staggered out the door.

"Hands up!"

"Get on the ground!"

The commands flew from the officers in rapid succession, losing any sense of coherence in his ears. He shuffled forward. Raising his hands above his head, he squeezed his eyes shut.

"Please don't shoot me!" Keilan shouted.

He took another step forward. Rebecca squeezed his shoulder, forcing him to stop. His eyes flew open to see the officers approaching. They continued shouting commands, their voices intermingling with a buzzing noise erupting in Keilan's ears. The noise grew louder, rising into a painful crescendo in his head. An enormous pressure built up, pressing outward on his skull. Keilan grabbed his ears and screamed.

Behind him, Rebecca held her arms out to her side, turning her palms toward the police officers. Blood seeped from the wounds in her hands, puddling on the concrete below. The drops sizzled as they hit the ground.

Slowly, she rose into the air. Her feet floated above the concrete as she drifted upward.

The buzzing in Keilan's ears stopped. His eyes flew open and he saw his own fear reflected in the officer's eyes.

"What the fuck?" One of the officers asked.

Keilan spun around. Rebecca continued rising off the ground, arms outstretched. Her bare feet were now at his eye level. He stumbled backward toward the police officers.

"I am Asmodeus!" The demon shouted in Rebecca's voice. It stopped rising and threw its head back. In a deep, booming voice, it spoke again. "And I've come to seduce the world!"

The ringing in Keilan's ears broke out again, causing him to collapse to his knees. A brutal pulsating broke out in his brain. His fingers dug into his temples, his nails tearing at the skin on the side of his head. He threw his head back, screaming for relief. The pounding grew stronger, threatening to crack his skull.

Keilan's head exploded, scattering shards of bone and brain matter in every direction. A splattering of blood coated Rebecca's face. She dragged her fingers across her forehead, gathering the blood onto her finger. Slipping the tip of her finger into her mouth, she sucked the blood off of it.

Rebecca's head snapped forward again. She glared at the officers with hatred in her eyes. Slowly, she descended toward the ground until the tips of her toes scraped against the concrete.

"Get... get on the ground." One of the officers stammered. "I'll shoot you."

Rebecca smiled. "I'm counting on it." Without warning, she accelerated toward the officers. Her toes floated over Keilan's dead body.

The officers retreated away from her, shouting commands. Rebecca grew closer, brandishing her teeth.

A single gunshot filled the air.

The officer closest to Rebecca stared at the pistol in his hand as if he couldn't believe it had gone off. His hands shook uncontrollably against the weight of the pistol. His eyes drifted from the barrel of his gun to Rebecca.

Rebecca was staring down at her nightgown. Blood spewed from a single hole in the center of her chest. Looking back up at the officers, she smiled.

"Now everyone will believe." Asmodeus whispered in Rebecca's voice.

Rebecca fell out of the sky, collapsing into a crumpled heap on the ground.

The officers approached the body, guns drawn. "I had to." Officer Brown insisted. "She was coming right at me." Officer Watson placed a hand on his back. "You saw that, right?" Brown said as he took a step forward and nudged Rebecca's body with his boot. "Is she dead?" He asked.

Officer Watson removed his hand from his partner's shoulder and stepped forward. Squatting down next to Rebecca, he placed his fingers against her neck. The three officers remained completely still, awaiting the verdict.

Watson nodded. "Yeah, she's dead." He said, removing his hand from her neck.

"Oh, fuck. Oh, fuck." Brown muttered.

"Don't worry, man. We got it all on our body cams." Watson said, tapping the camera attached to his chest. "It's all on video, anyone can see it."

The third officer approached and looked from the other two officers to the dead girl. "Who the fuck is Asmodeus?"

"A demon..." Officer Brown whispered. He quickly crossed himself and said a prayer.

The Empty Crib

Peter eased the Honda Odyssey into the driveway, taking the steep incline more gently than he usually would. He grimaced as the vehicle went over the small bump at the base of the parking pad. His eyes instinctively shot to his wife. Peter expected her to make some sort of noise or brace herself against the jolt, but she swayed with the motion of the car, completely devoid of expression. Operating on autopilot, he shifted the minivan into park and depressed the ignition button. Their nearly new vehicle fell silent.

"Are you ready?" Peter whispered. He sucked in a deep breath before turning his head to face his wife.

Amy's already pale skin appeared translucent in the dying light of sunset. Her sunken eyes burned a furious red, evidence of the hours spent crying. Dark blue bags hung from her bottom eyelids. She hadn't bothered to brush her hair, instead allowing a nurse to wrap it into a messy bun.

She didn't seem to hear him. She continued staring through the windshield toward their house. Peter followed her gaze to the window on the second floor. He sighed and pushed open his door.

Exiting the car, Peter could feel the cold air lick at his skin with each gust. The grass in the front yard was well above its usual height and the HOA would no doubt be sending him a nasty letter soon. He grunted at the thought, far too tired to mow the lawn, and more than willing to pay the fine.

Peter turned away from his unkempt yard and moved around to his wife's door. He tugged at the handle but it didn't budge.

"Fuck." Peter muttered as he fished the keys out of his pocket. Amy watched as he struggled to retrieve the key fob but made no move to unlock her door. Normally, her lack of assistance would have infuriated him and probably launched them into a tirade of insults. This time, he understood.

Dutifully, he wrestled with his pocket and pulled out the key fob. Clicking the unlock button twice, the sound of the car's locks releasing told him it was safe to try the door again. He pulled, and this time it opened with ease.

Amy still didn't look at him. She wore the vacant expression of a dead body, her eyes transfixed on that bedroom window.

Peter reached into the car, sliding his hands into her armpits.

"Come on, babe. Let's get you inside." He said, grunting as he strained to hoist her to her feet. Amy barely helped, allowing her dead weight to fall onto his shoulders and forcing him to fight gravity. To his relief, she voluntarily put her feet on the ground and stood up, taking the pressure off his aching back. He wrapped her arm around his shoulders and placed one hand on her hip. Together, they limped toward the front door.

The front door of the Watson house flew open. Margery Watson poked her head out, wearing an enormous grin.

"Let me see that baby!" She shouted at the couple. The old woman emerged from her home and power walked across the front lawn adjoining the two homes. She clapped enthusiastically as she approached but stopped about twenty feet away. Her clapping halted, her hands flying to her mouth. A look of realization dawned on her face.

Peter slowly shook his head, hoping she would take his invitation to fuck off with some grace. The woman continued her approach at a much slower pace. Inhaling deeply, Peter prepared for a confrontation.

"Oh, my god!" She got within touching distance of the couple. "What happened?"

Tears erupted from Amy's eyes before Margery even finished her question. Her knees quivered and her body heaved with a violent sob. She slumped against her husband, allowing him to support her full weight.

A tidal wave of anger washed over Peter. He glanced at his sobbing wife, then back at Mrs. Watson. All of the anger, hurt, disappointment and despair he had experienced over the last seventy-two hours exploded to the surface like a volcano. Before he could stop himself, he lashed out at the well-meaning old lady.

"What does it look like, Margery?" He snapped. She recoiled at his bite, or maybe it was his familiar use of her first name. He had always taken great care to show the elderly couple respect. He even started mowing their lawn when Mr. Waton wasn't capable anymore. All those years of carefully cultivating his reputation within the neighborhood were washed away in seconds, and he couldn't care less. "Do you see a fucking baby in our arms?"

Mrs. Watson took a tentative step back. "I'm so sorry." She whispered, her arms outstretched in a surrendering motion.

Amy squeezed Peter's hand. The overwhelming wave of emotions washed back out to sea, leaving him with only embarrassment. His face flushed red as his senses returned. "No." He sighed. "I'm so sorry, Mrs. Watson. You didn't deserve that."

Tears welled in the old woman's eyes. She reached out and placed a shaking hand on his shoulder. "That's ok, Peter. I understand."

Peter looked away, unable to tolerate seeing his own pain mirrored in her eyes. "Look, Mrs. Watson, I appreciate you coming out here, but I'm going to get Amy inside. Ok?"

"Of course, dear." Margery patted his shoulder again. "You just holler if you need anything." She withdrew her hand from his shoulder and pointed a bony finger at him. "I mean it, Peter. If you need anything at all."

Peter nodded. "Yes, Ma'am. Thank you." He turned away from her and continued escorting his wife through their front door.

Amy made no attempt to resist or assist. Peter operated his wife like a puppeteer working with his marionette. He whispered commands such as, "step up" or "easy now," in her ear, and she obeyed. Things got tougher once they were inside the house. The couple navigated their way through the living room, carefully avoiding the wooden coffee table that Peter was prone to banging his shins against.

Peter let out a deep exhale when they reached the stairs. The wooden steps reached up into the utterly dark hallway above. He risked releasing one of his hands from around his wife's hip and smacked it against the wall. The knock of his hand against the drywall echoed through the house several more times until his fingers brushed against the light switch. The click of the switch replaced the echoes. Then, a subtle hum buzzed as the light above the stairs came to life.

"Ok, babe." Peter said. He slid his hand back around her waist. "This is going to be tough. I need you to help me out a bit."

Slowly, Amy nodded.

Peter's heart soared. That was the first sign of life she had given since they had left the hospital. For the briefest moment in time, he had hope that they would pull through this. Amy withdrew her hand from around her husband's shoulders and gripped the banister. Tugging with her arms, she tentatively climbed the first step. Peter's hands slid from her shoulders down to his wife's hips, hoping to balance her as she walked. He followed her up the stairs, careful to maintain a wide stance so he could catch her if she fell.

Using the handrails on either side of the stairs, Amy pulled herself along. She grunted in pain with each step.

The couple lost all track of time as they crept up the stairs. After what seemed like an hour, they reached the second floor, where the hallway stretched out in front of them, with two closed doors at the end.

Amy used her hands as guides. She pressed them firmly against the wall and staggered down the hallway. They brushed roughly against the drywall, coming dangerously close to the assortment of decorations lining the wall. Peter followed close behind, his hands outstretched, ready to grab her at a moment's notice.

Without warning, Amy came to an abrupt stop. It caught Peter completely by surprise, and he almost crashed into her. Going onto his tiptoes, he stopped his momentum.

He was about to ask her why she had stopped when he realized she was staring at the wall. He followed her gaze to a large picture frame. It was a photo of a very pregnant Amy in a flowery dress. The dress stretched out behind her, carried away by the wind. Her hands rested on her protruding stomach. A sun flare streaked across the top of the image. It was the one photo of her pregnancy that Amy truly loved. She used to joke that it was the only photo that didn't make her look like a sad cow.

A tear worked its way from the corner of Amy's eye. The single droplet carved a moist path down her cheek.

It reached her chin and desperately clung there until Peter reached out and wiped the tear away. His eyes drifted down to where Amy's hands had left the wall. They rested protectively against her now flattened stomach.

"Come on, babe." Peter encouraged. He returned his hands to her hips and guided her toward their closed bedroom door. Her eyes lingered on the picture as long as they could, only flicking away when it was totally obscured from view. When they reached their closed bedroom door, Peter gently reached around his wife and pushed it open.

The room was completely dark, save for a single beam of sunlight cutting a path through a crack in the curtains. Peter continued guiding Amy to the bed, where he peeled back the covers. Without waiting for Peter's instructions, she gently climbed into the bed, a slight pain-filled moan escaping her lips. Her face contorted into a grimace as she lowered herself onto the pillow, turning into a fetal position. Peter tugged on the covers, bringing them all the way to Amy's chin. He leaned close to her, his lips brushing her ear.

"I love you."

Amy didn't respond. Peter lingered there a moment longer before relenting. He rushed around the edge of the bed and yanked the curtain closed, plummeting the room into complete darkness.

He climbed into the bed next to his distraught wife and allowed its warmth to swallow him. His head sunk into the pillow, the clutches of sleep immediately sinking its claws into him.

Amy lay there staring into the darkness. Her eyes slowly adjusted, allowing her to make out the vague outline of her husband. His slow, rhythmic breathing told her he had fallen asleep. A burning rage tore through her. She couldn't believe he could come in and fall asleep without any trouble. Meanwhile, the anguish she felt caused a knot to form in her stomach that wouldn't allow her to get comfortable. A tear rolled down her face and soaked into the pillow. She squeezed her eyes together, desperate to fight through the tears. Her eyes burned from a combination of crying and lack of sleep. As she lay there, she feared she might never have a good night's rest again. Rolling onto her back, Amy released a quiet groan. Pain carved a hot path across her groin and into her abdomen. Another tear rolled off her face. She had prepared herself for the pain childbirth would bring, and anticipated the discomfort, and she had plunged headfirst into that pain anticipation. More tears rolled down her face. She would take all that pain and more for one more chance to hold her baby. That single thought burrowed into her mind. She just wanted to hold her baby.

She was about to roll over and try to get some sleep when a faint rustling noise from somewhere in the house caught her attention. It sounded like someone moving around in the hallway. Holding her breath, she cocked her head, searching for another sound. Beside her, Peter continued rhythmically breathing, completely unaware of the disturbance. She exhaled slowly, trying to calm her nerves.

"It's just your mind playing tricks on you." She whispered. The combination of surgery, pain medication and heartbreak clouded her mind. Rolling onto her side, she pulled the covers back up to her chin and closed her eyes.

A baby's wail filled the air.

Amy's blood ran cold. Goosebumps rippled their way across her back. Ignoring the searing pain in her stomach, she pushed herself into a seated position and tried to stand up.

Her legs weakened under her weight, sending her crashing to the floor. Pain exploded through her groin. Warm liquid flooded her lower body. She instinctively reached for her belly only for her hands to come away bloody. She gasped when the baby cried again.

"Peter!" She cried. "Peter, please wake up."

Peter flew out of bed like it was on fire. "What? What's wrong?" He asked as he rushed around to her side of the bed. She could hear him fumbling against the wall, search-ing for the light switch.

The room exploded into light. Amy shielded her eyes from the brightness, covering her face in her own blood in the process.

"Oh, my God!" Peter shouted. He scrambled to her side and dropped to his knees. They crashed into the wood floor with a painful thud but he didn't acknowledge it. His hands flew to her shirt and yanked it up, revealing the soaked-through bandage across her belly. "It's ok, baby." He insisted. He quickly patted down his pockets, search-ing for his cell phone. "I'll call an ambulance."

"No!" Amy shouted. Her face stretched into a look of desperation. "The baby!" She yelled.

Peter recoiled at her outburst. Sadness replaced the look of fear he was wearing. "Baby." He whispered. Reaching up, he squeezed her shoulder. "Amy, the baby is gone." He said as gently as he could.

She shook her head. "There's a baby in the house." She said. "I heard it crying!"

Peter's eyebrows furrowed, causing the wrinkles in his forehead to deepen. His hand fell away from her shoulder and rested on his knee. Shaking his head, he reached under her armpits and hoisted her to her feet with a grunt.

A hot poker of fiery pain stabbed into her groin. Her eyes involuntarily clenched against the sensation. She bit into her lip to keep from screaming, drawing a few droplets of blood in the process. Peter positioned her over the bed and let go. She fell helplessly onto the bed, her abdominal muscles quickly giving out. A squeal escaped her lips when her head hit the pillow. The hot poker worked its way from her groin to her stomach, searing a hole through her insides. Tears broke free and plummeted down her face.

"There's no baby." Peter chided. He grabbed the covers and yanked them up to her chin, more forcefully than he had the first time.

Amy stared up at her husband, a look of disgust mirrored in her eyes. The burning pain in her stomach subsided, only to be replaced with a different kind of hurt. She couldn't understand why he was acting this way. Peter had always been the model husband, the kind of guy she would brag about to her friends. He was the husband that made the other wives jealous. Yet, here he was, being aggressive with her in her weakest moment.

The anger and disgust on his face softened as he stared down at his helpless wife. "I'm sorry, babe." He whispered. Leaning down, he kissed her on the forehead. Using the bottom of his shirt, he wiped the blood from her cheek. "I'm just tired and hurt. I shouldn't have taken that out on you." The tone of his voice seemed genuine to Amy, who simply nodded. She didn't trust herself not to break out in sobs.

"Would it make you feel better if I checked the house?" He asked and threw a thumb over his shoulder. Amy nodded and without another word, Peter retreated from the room.

Amy listened to the sounds of Peter stomping down the hall. The nursery door was thrown open, followed by a moment of silence, then the patter of his bare feet smacking against the stairs. After another minute, she heard him climbing the steps and speed-walking toward their bedroom. He appeared in their open doorway, shaking his head.

"There's nobody here, babe."

Amy squeezed her eyes, fighting the tears away. "Thank you for checking."

Peter flipped the light switch, launching the room back into darkness. He moved around to his side of the bed and climbed in. Gently, so as to not hurt his wife, he scooted closer to her and wrapped an arm around her waist.

"We're going to get through this." He whispered.

"I really thought I heard a baby crying." Amy said.

Peter kissed the base of her neck. "I know. It's ok, babe."

Amy rolled onto her back. Staring at the ceiling, she willed herself to fall asleep. Within a few minutes, Peter's slow, rhythmic breathing returned and Amy was once again alone with her thoughts. Images from the hospital flashed in her mind. Scenes of doctors rushing in and out of the room were drowned out by Peter's frantic cries. She heard his voice echoing in her mind.

"Just save the baby."

That's what he wanted. Between her and the baby, he had chosen the baby. She wanted to hate him for that, but in truth, she didn't blame him. Her memory of the events was cloudy, but she was pretty sure she had begged the doctors to save the baby as they wheeled her into the operating room.

Her eyelids grew heavy and threatened to close. A stream of light broke through the window and covered the ceiling with shadows. Amy watched them shift as a car drove by, desperately trying to push the horrific hospital scenes from her mind. She was nearly asleep when one of the shadows moved.

Her heart froze in place. A fist-sized knot formed in her stomach. It was the outline of a baby. Its shadow crawled across the ceiling, stopping directly above her. Amy's pulse quickened, her heart slamming against the walls of her chest. The shadow lingered above her, not moving.

Outside, the car rumbled down the road, reflecting more light into the room and washing away the shadow. Amy stared at the spot in the ceiling but the shadow didn't return. A tear broke free from the corner of her eye and rolled down to her ear. Her bottom lip quivered. Covering her mouth with her hand, she bit down hard on her lip. Afraid to wake up Peter a second time, she stifled the sobs.

A beep filled the air. Then another.

The sound caught Amy off guard and she nearly screamed in surprise. Glancing around the room, she couldn't see what was making the sound.

Another beep.

The beeps were growing louder and faster now. She heard people shouting. Her head snapped over to Peter. He was still soundly asleep. His snores rose up to challenge the screams.

The bathroom light flicked on. Its beams streaked out through the crack between the bottom of the door and the floor. The screams grew louder. The incessant beeping lost its rhythm. The frantic screams morphed into cries for help.

Amy listened, glued to the bed, paralyzed by fear. The cries and screams sounded familiar. She strained her ears to listen until the voice screamed out Peter's name. It was her voice.

Goosebumps broke out across Amy's skin. The petrifying fear released its hold on her. Unable to sit up, she rolled off the bed. Pain radiated out from her abdomen as she struggled to get her feet underneath her. Using the edge of the bed, she pushed herself upright and staggered through the darkness toward the bathroom. The light bursting from under the door grew brighter as she approached, morphing from the yellowish glow of bathroom lights to the sterilizing white lights of an operating room. The screams grew loud enough to shake the walls. Tentatively, she reached out for the handle. Inhaling deeply, she turned the knob and pushed.

Squinting against the blinding lights, she saw it all. The operating room. Her reddening face as blood gushed from between her legs, painting the floor in a viscous red. Doctors ran around the room, screaming at one another. Peter's pale face as he slumped against the wall. She closed her eyes, nausea rising in her stomach.

When she opened her eyes, the screaming stopped, and she stared into the dark bathroom. The horrific scene had literally vanished in the blink of an eye.

Amy scrambled forward, the nausea in her stomach winning out. She propelled herself to the floor and heaved into the open toilet. She could feel the stitches in her stomach tearing from the violent abdominal contractions.

Moving as quietly as possible so as to not wake Peter, she cleaned her mouth with a hand towel and flushed the toilet. She wiped her face again, soaking up a stream of tears. Her mind raced. It had all seemed so real to her. She couldn't understand what had happened. Her fingers combed through her hair, fingernails digging deep into her scalp.

She retreated from the bathroom, the warm trickle of blood dripping down the inside of her left thigh. The bathroom door clicked closed louder than Amy had intended. She winced, waiting for Peter to wake up. His snoring morphed into a grunt. The bed springs moaned as he rolled over. She froze until his snoring resumed its steady pace.

Amy contemplated her options. There was no way she would be able to fall asleep now. Pain seared through her stomach and groin, her heart was still beating out of her chest and her mind raced. She settled on a glass of water and some more pain pills.

Tiptoeing across the bedroom, she reached the door and slipped out into the hallway. The door to the nursery stared her directly in the face. The name Tyler was displayed prominently in different colored letters. It was a small feature, but it meant the world to Amy. She had always dreamt of having a home with the kids' names on the doors. Now, that's all it ever would be: a dream. A dream that died with her child.

Subconsciously, she reached out for the doorknob but stopped short. Amy knew she wasn't ready. Shaking her head, Amy forced herself to turn away from the nursery door. The floorboards creaked under her weight, a single night light at the end of the hall was her only source of light. She reached the top of the stairs and took the first step. The pain in her abdomen grew worse. She braced for the next step when a baby's cry erupted from within the nursery.

Amy spun around. Her eyes were transfixed on the nursery doors, reading the name of her dead son over and over again. She willed her ears to hear the sound again and prayed to a God she no longer believed in to convince her the noise was real.

Another cry.

This one was full of pain and panic. Amy's heart exploded through her chest. Her baby was in trouble. She leaped up the last stair and sprinted down the hallway. The door exploded open under her weight, sending the letters of Tyler's name sprawling across the floor. She peered into the darkened room, scanning for the source of the crying.

Another cry erupted from the crib. She rushed across the room, leaving a trail of bloody footprints in her wake.

More blood gushed from her groin and the torn stitches in her stomach. She ignored the searing pain and tossed herself against the crib. Her fingers danced frantically through the blankets and pillows in search of the crying baby. She launched the items over her shoulder, expelling them from the crib until it was completely empty.

The cries continued. They swirled around her. Tyler's wails drifted in and out of her ears. They reverberated off the walls.

"Please!" She yelled. "Let me help you!" She leaned against the crib, allowing it to support her full weight and screamed. Her shout ejected all of her emotions. It was full of pain, anger, dejection, and disappointment. She screamed again before falling into hysterics.

"What the fuck are you doing?" Peter shouted.

Amy whirled around to see Peter looming in the doorway. She stumbled toward him. Blood freely poured from her stomach now. It flooded her shirt and waterfalled to the floor.

"I heard him, Peter." She wailed. "Tyler was crying for me."

Peter stared at his wife. The night light in the hallway silhouetted him in the door frame. "Tyler's dead." Peter growled.

Amy shook her head. "No, Peter. I can hear him." She pointed a shaky finger at the crib. "I can hear him in the crib."

She was close enough now to see her husband's face. Instead of the sympathetic or loving face she expected, his face was contorted into a look of hatred.

"There's nothing in that crib." Peter sneered.

"Peter, please listen to me." Amy begged. She collapsed to the ground in front of him. He made no move to help her. She looked up into the hate-filled face of her husband as he gazed down. His lip turned up into a look of disgust. Amy reached out and took his hands with her own blood-soaked fingers.

With one shove, he tossed her aside. Amy slumped to the floor. She tried to prop herself up on her hands but slipped in the blood seeping from her wounds. Her head smacked off the floor and she shrieked in pain.

Peter stepped over her and strutted toward the crib. Tyler's cries grew louder with each step, growing into a crescendo when Peter reached the crib.

"I should have thrown this shit out the moment our son died." Peter said sternly. "Waste of fucking space now, don't you think?"

Tyler's panicked wails pierced Amy's ears. They were too loud. Her eardrums felt as if they would explode at any second. Under the unrelenting pressure, she clawed at her ears, desperate for a respite from the pain.

Peter cocked his hand back and punched one of the white spokes of the crib. The wood shattered under the assault. Before Amy could react, he swung again, another spoke breaking free and crashing against the wall.

"Peter! No!" Amy screamed at her husband's back. He either didn't hear her or didn't care. He cocked back his fist again and brought it down, splintering the wood crib.

Amy crawled across the floor through her own blood. She reached her husband's legs. Using the waistband of his shorts, she climbed up his bare legs, clawing at his skin.

"Please, Peter! I'm begging you!" She sobbed. Tyler's cries were unbearable now. They bounced off the walls, increasing the pressure in her head with every passing second. White spots appeared in her vision. "Please!"

Her pleas didn't seem to register. He continued his barbaric attack on the crib. Pieces of wood scattered across the floor.

Amy punched desperately at her husband's legs and ass, willing herself to gather enough strength to stop him.

"Please!" She cried in one last desperate attempt to salvage her baby's bed.

Throwing his leg back, Peter kicked Amy off of him. She tumbled to the floor. Another hot prong of pain seared its way through her body. She gasped for air.

Tyler's cries grew fainter with each savage strike against the crib. Amy knew the strikes were killing her baby all over again. She wailed on the floor, clenching her stomach. Her eyes scanned the area, looking for any way to stop Peter. She felt around behind her. Her fingers brushed over splinters of wood before finding purchase on one of the broken spokes. Without thinking, she grasped it and swung.

The broken part of the wood slammed into Peter's calf. His skin shredded against the jagged wood tips. The hunk of wood tore through the muscle of his calf. Blood exploded from the wound, coating Amy's face in a red spray.

Peter screamed. He stared down at his injured leg in disbelief. His nostrils flared as he reached down and grabbed the part of the wood still sticking out of his skin. With a hard tug, he yanked the wood out of his calf. It came away with a sickening swoosh. Blood seeped from the wound and rolled down his calf. It pooled around his foot and intermixed with Amy's blood.

"You stupid, fucking cunt!" He shouted. Peter tossed himself onto his wife. His fingers closed around a clump of her hair. He hoisted her head off the ground and brought her close to eye level. With his other hand, Peter pointed at the destroyed crib. "Tyler isn't in there!"

His muscles tightened and he smashed her head against the wood floor. Stars danced in Amy's eyes. She fought against the encroaching darkness at the corners of her vision.

"Peter, please!" She begged.

"This is all your fault!" He screamed into her face. Spittle flew from his lips and coated her forehead. "You had one fucking job and you couldn't do it!" He smacked her head into the ground again. Amy clawed at his face, tearing the skin across his cheek and drawing a few droplets of blood. "There's nothing in this fucking room!" He shouted, seemingly oblivious to the new cuts on his face.

He lifted her again. Amy knew she wouldn't remain conscious after a third blow. Her eyes desperately scanned for anything to defend herself with.

Another of the broken wooden spokes reached out to her from the ruined crib. Without thinking, she grabbed it and swung.

The wood embedded itself in Peter's neck. He released a gurgled choking sound. His fingers uncurled from her hair and she slumped to the floor. His eyes stretched wide and his hands flew to the open wound. Every few seconds, blood spurted from the wound, repainting the white crib.

Amy watched in horror as he stumbled backward against the bookshelf. One of the shelves collapsed under the impact, sending several books crashing to the floor. Peter tried to crawl out of the room. Blood spurted in every direction, creating a sickly soup on the floor of the nursery. He made it a few feet before falling flat onto his stomach. His legs twitched and scraped against the wooden floor, searching for traction to continue driving him forward.

Amy squealed with tears gushing down her face. Peter quit moving.

"Peter?" Amy asked softly. "Peter?"

Amy's hands flew to her mouth. "Oh my God." She quivered uncontrollably. "What have I done?"

Ignoring the searing pain in her stomach, she pushed herself onto all fours and crawled to her husband. She rested a hand on his shoulder and shook him. "Peter? Peter, wake up." She commanded. "Peter?" She screamed.

Her scream was met by the calming sound of a baby cooing. Amy's head snapped around to see a baby lying naked in the previously empty crib.

"Tyler?" She whispered. She crawled across the room. The broken splinters of wood stabbed at her knees and hands. She pushed through the pain, continuing to ignore the blood pouring from her wound.

She approached the baby and reached out to it, caressing its tender skin. The baby returned her touch with a toothless grin.

Slowly, the darkness continued encroaching on her vision until the baby faded from sight. Overwhelming fatigue washed over her. Amy lowered her head, her finger still caressing the baby as she slipped into unconsciousness.

"Deputy Blackburn, Tall Oak Sheriff's Office." Joshua Blackburn announced himself while opening the front door. "I'm here to do a wellness check on Amy and Peter Talbert!" He pushed the door open a little wider. The gut-wrenching stench of death smacked the deputy in the face and filled his nostrils. He buried his nose into the crook of his elbow and backed away from the open door. Fighting back a gag, he depressed a button on his radio. Behind him, Margery Watson gagged and retreated off the porch. Holding up his hand to her, he said, "Stay here."

"Deputy Blackburn to dispatch. I got a signal seven." He said into the radio. "Roll more units to my location." He released the button on his radio and pushed the door fully open. Death permeated the air and wafted from the open doorway. Deputy Blackburn drew his pistol from its holster and held it out in front of him while he entered the house. He checked room by room on the first floor, scanning for threats and any sign of the dead body.

When he reached the staircase, the malodor grew stronger. "Deputy Blackburn with the Tall Oak Sheriff's Office. I'm coming up." He called out. The deputy took the stairs slowly, gently placing one foot in front of the other while keeping his gun and eyes trained on the landing at the top.

The hallway was illuminated by a single nightlight. He paused to scan the area and noticed the light glinting off a liquid at the end of the hall. It seemed to seep out from underneath a closed door. Deputy Blackburn tightened his grip on the pistol and crept down the hall, pausing in front of the door. The letter "T" dangled from a single nail, the remaining letters were missing. A shudder rolled down the deputy's back.

"This is Deputy Blackburn. Last chance to come out." He called. Waiting a moment for a response that never came, he reached out with his free hand and turned the knob. Taking a deep breath, he exploded through the door.

The carnage before him came to him in fragmented pieces. The dead man, face down on the ground with a chunk of wood protruding from his neck. Blood spatter decorated the walls of the nursery. A shattered crib lay empty against the far wall. A woman in a pool for her own blood, the stitched-up wound of a cesarean section violently torn open.

His mind put the fragments together and constructed the image before him, then grabbed his radio and pressed the button. "Dispatch, I got a signal seven, times two. Run me homicide and some backup."

He re-holstered his pistol and covered his nose. Backing out of the room slowly, he turned to leave.

Then he heard it.

A baby crying in the nursery.

Blue Eyes

Marian pulled the comb through Anna's hair, marveling at how the three-year-old managed to get it so tangled during the course of the day. It became lodged in an impossible nest at the back of the little girl's head. Anna whined as the bristles ripped through the knotted mess. She covered her face to hide the tears building up in the corners of her eyes.

"Quit whining, we're almost done." Marian commanded. She tugged harder, trying to dislodge the brush. The sound of tearing hair filled the bathroom.

"Mommy, it hurts." The little girl complained through her hands.

Marian looked at her daughter's reflection in the mirror. She could see her daughter peeking through her fingers. Enormous alligator tears spilled from her bright blue eyes and ran down her cheeks. Marian sighed and opened a drawer to retrieve the detangling spray.

Holding it out for Anna to see, she said, "We'll try some more of this, ok?" Anna nodded eagerly. "Now, wipe those tears so I can see your beautiful blue eyes."

A huge smile stretched across Anna's face, revealing the big gap between her teeth. She was so excited for that gap because it meant she would get her first set of grown-up teeth soon. Plus, it meant the tooth fairy would be paying her a visit soon.

The bathroom door clicked shut, drawing both of their attention away from the mirror. Elsa stood in the entryway, her hair already brushed and pulled back over her shoulders. The oversized nightgown she wore dangled to the floor, depicting her favorite Disney princess, Ariel. The mermaid floated in the water with her friends, her bright blue eyes matching her radiant smile.

She stood with her shoulders slumped, looking down at her nightgown. "I wish I had blue eyes, Mommy." Elsa said. She absentmindedly rubbed her pointer finger along the lines of Ariel's eyes. "They're so pretty." Now, it was her turn to start crying.

Marian sat the brush down on the counter and looked toward the ceiling. This prolonged bedtime routine was becoming an all too common occurrence in their household, and she was growing sick of it. Elsa had been complaining for a few weeks about having brown eyes like her father. Marian tried several tactics to set the young girl at ease. She tried praising her eyes as beautiful and showing her photos of her brown-eyed grandmother. When that didn't work, she even tried to explain genetics several times, but the concept eluded her six-year-old's brain.

With an exasperated sigh, Marian turned to face her daughter. "We've been over this, baby. Your brown eyes are beautiful." She moved over to her oldest daughter and squatted down in front of her. Gripping her daughter's tiny shoulders, she held her at arm's length. She opened her mouth to speak but paused. Adjusting her gaze, she looked directly into her daughter's eyes. "They remind me so much of your father's. Do you know where he got them?" The little girl nodded her head, her recently brushed blonde hair waving about. "He got them from his mother, your grandmother." Marian continued. "Do you remember the picture I showed you?" Again, the young girl nodded. "She was so beautiful and you look just like her!" Marian gave her daughter a reassuring smile before pulling her into a tight embrace. After a moment, Marian rubbed Elsa's back and stood up. She moved back to Anna and continued brushing her hair.

"But I don't look like you." Elsa protested after a minute. "And Anna does. That's not fair."

Marian gave up on trying to break through the knot and threw open the drawer again. She pulled out a small pair of scissors. The scissors were normally used for cutting cuticles and minor grooming, but Marian supposed it would work for hair as well. Sliding it into her daughter's hair, she carefully clipped at the knot until she was able to pull it free. Once the knot was gone, she tossed the scissors onto the counter and sighed again. It was times like this that she regretted letting Alex take the overnight shift at the Sheriff's office. He was making more money, but it left her alone, functioning as a single mother. "Sweetie, you're beautiful. The color of your eyes wouldn't change that. Plus, there's nothing we could do about that, right?" She said without looking at Elsa.

"We could get me blue eyes." Elsa suggested.

Marian put her hands on her hips. "And just how would we do that?" She regretted feeding into this tangent as soon as the words left her mouth. Marian's patience was hanging on by a thread now.

"We could get something sharp and cut them out?" The words came out in a sweet and hopeful tone, making the violent suggestion sound even more ominous. Elsa gazed up at her mom with hopeful eyes.

Marian whirled around. "Elsa! That's horrible! Don't ever say anything like that again!" Marian scolded. "That's so violent. What would make you say something like that?"

The girl took a subtle step back and began to tear up. "I just want to have beautiful eyes like you, mommy." She wrapped her hand around herself in a self-hug.

"We've been over this a thousand times. Your eyes are beautiful the way they are. Now, I don't want to hear about this again." She turned away from her daughters and ran a hand through her own unkempt hair. "It's bedtime. Let's go, both of you." She said as she spun back toward the girls.

She ushered the girls out of the bathroom and into their shared room. When her and Alex decided she would be a stay-at-home mom, they had to downsize their house, resulting in the girls sharing a room. It was a point of contention in their marriage. Marian felt each girl needed their own space to develop their own identity. Alex said they'd figure it out, and it wasn't possible until he became a detective. Just as she had feared, he made detective, and they were still in a two-bedroom house.

The girls exploded into their room and rushed to their respective beds. Like every night, Marian tucked Anna in first, pulling the covers up to her daughter's chin. The little girl gazed up at her with those fierce blue eyes. Marian couldn't help but admire the girl's beauty. It was a vain thought since Anna really was the spitting image of her, but she couldn't help it. They both had blonde hair, a rounded face and a pointy nose. And their eyes. She kissed her daughter on the tip of her nose and exchanged "good nights" and "sweet dreams."

She turned to her other daughter, who was sitting up in bed. Marian got down on her knees and cupped her daughter's chin with both hands. Forcing Elsa's gaze up to meet her own, she put on the most compassionate look she could manage. "You are a beautiful young lady. Your eyes are beautiful and there is no reason not to like them." Elsa reluctantly nodded and laid down. Marian patted her daughter on the head and tucked her into the covers, kissing her on the tip of her nose. She crept to the door. Pausing with her finger on the light switch, she took one last look at the girls, both totally obsessed with them and so grateful they were going to bed. Flipping off the light, she retreated from the room.

With both kids finally asleep, Marian returned to the bathroom for her own nightly routine. She brushed her teeth and combed her hair before changing into her own nightgown. As she leaves the bathroom, she notices a single strand of fabric hanging from the sleeve. Turning back to the counter, she reached for the scissors she had left on the counter, but they weren't there. She scanned her messy countertop, moving aside her straightener, a palette of makeup, and a box of fake lashes. There was nothing on the floor besides a dirt towel, which she moved around with her foot just to verify it wasn't in there. She opened the drawer and shuffled through it for a moment. It wasn't there either. Sighing, she closed the drawer and cursed herself for being so forgetful. Her eyelids had grown heavy since putting the kids to bed and she resolved to find the scissors the next day. She wrapped the little strand of fabric around her finger and snapped it off. It fell gently to the floor. Marian threw herself into bed, pulling the covers to her chin and flipping off the lamp on her nightstand. She made a mental note to clean her bathroom tomorrow. Her phone chirped. Without looking, she knew it was her husband's goodnight text. Glancing at the time, She smiled. Ten on the dot.

Goodnight Blue Eyes Love You

Her fingers danced across the keyboard. Firing off a goodnight text of her own, she plugged the phone in and sank into her pillow. Within minutes, sleep dug its claws into her, and she drifted off.

"Mommy." The soft whisper stirred Marian from what had been a peaceful dream. She rubbed her eyes and glanced at the LED clock on her bedside table.

3:15 AM

"Mommy?" Elsa's little voice asked again. Something about the tone of her voice sent shivers down her spine. It didn't sound groggy like a girl waking up from a nightmare. Marian's drowsy brain searched for a word to describe it. Her voice sounded...pained.

"Yes, baby?" Marian asked, her throat hoarse from snoring.

"I have blue eyes."

Marian's eyes snapped open. "What?" She shot up in bed. The streetlight outside of her window illuminated enough of the room so she could see the outline of her daughter standing in the doorway. She swayed back and forth, shrouded in darkness. The little girl took a half step forward, nearly losing her balance in the process. A knot formed in the pit of Marian's stomach.

"I have blue eyes like you, Mommy." The little girl sniffled a bit as she spoke. Marian was sure now. She could hear pain in Elsa's voice.

Marian scrambled for the lamp on her bedside. Her sleepy fingers danced clumsily against the assortment of objects on the table, sending several of them crashing to the floor. Her hands brushed against the top of the lamp several times before they found the switch. She flicked it, washing the room in bright fluorescent light. Turning back to her daughter, she inadvertently swung her arm wildly, knocking over a bottle of lotion. It fell from the table with a thud and rolled across the floor.

Marian tracked its path until it came to a stop at her daughter's feet. She slowly raised her eyes, taking in the scene before her in parts. Her mouth fell open as she fought for enough air to scream.

Blood coated her bare little feet. A trail of red footprints marked her path into the room. It coated her Ariel night-gown, staining the mermaid a deep shade of crimson and obscuring the sea creatures around her.

Marian's eyes flicked to the bloody pair of scissors in the girl's hand. The same pair of scissors she had used to get the knot out of Anna's hair. The same pair of scissors she had haphazardly left on the counter. The same pair she had searched for before bed. The same pair she couldn't find.

She traced the line of blood running up Elsa's arm to her face. When Marian finally saw Elsa's eyes, she screamed.

Elsa continued to sway, obviously struggling to stand upright. She had shredded her eyelids into strips of thin flesh. They shifted like curtains in the wind when she tried to blink. Blood seeped from all sides of her eyes, intermingling with the tears. It coated her forehead and cheeks, painting her red. And inside that bloody, massacred mess of a face sat two blue eyes. Her sister's eyes

"Now I look like you, Mommy."

The Dahlonega Reaper

Carlos eased the car off the highway and allowed the slight incline in the road to slow his vehicle down. The road narrowed before him, flanked on his left by enormous rocks. They raised up toward the sky like stone pillars, blocking out the surrounding countryside. On his right, the road ended abruptly at a cliff. It opened below him, giving him a nearly unobstructed view of the valley and the vast expanse of wilderness that stretched out below them. His heart rate quickened. Shifting in his seat, Carlos sat up a little straighter. He craned his neck to view over the hood, desperately trying to avoid getting too close to the edge.

Noticing her husband's discomfort, Maria reached over and rubbed his shoulder. She gave him a reassuring smile, then glanced into the rearview mirror at the kids. Luis had his nose buried in his tablet, probably shooting aliens, utterly oblivious to the change in scenery. Adrian leaned against his window. Maria watched as a streak of drool worked its way down his cheek and marred the clean windows. Camila's hand moved back and forth in rapid succession while she colored away in her coloring book.

"I'm going to stop at this gas station and fill up." Carlos said.

Maria leaned over and examined the dashboard. "You still have half a tank."

Carlos shook his head. "It's a long way up the mountain." He stole a glance at his wife, then immediately returned his gaze to the road. "I don't want to risk it." He muttered as he squeezed the steering wheel a little tighter.

He threw on the blinker and pulled up to a pump. Stepping out of the car, he leaned back into the driver's side. "I'm going to grab a coffee while I'm in there. You want anything?" Maria shook her head. He blew her a kiss, then pushed himself off the car.

Carlos jogged across the empty parking lot and up to the building. An old Coke sign covered in dust hung in the window, flanked on either side by signs for local beers. Brown stains streaked across the metal roof and deep cracks ran down the walls.

The inside of the store wasn't much better. A single long light fixture hung from the ceiling and stretched down the center of the tiny store. There was a single shelving unit covered in expired snacks. Carlos looked around for any sign of a coffee machine but didn't see one.

"Can I help you?" A woman's deep voice asked. Carlos cringed at the sound of it. There was a crackle in her lungs. It sounded as if the woman had smoked three packs a day for the last forty years. Shaking off the uncomfortable feeling the old lady's voice gave him, he threw on a smile.

"Yes, ma'am. I was hoping to get some coffee." He said.

The woman looked him over with her deep, sunken eyes. The wrinkles on her face and the yellow tint to her hands confirmed that she was, in fact, a smoker. A nearly empty pack of Pall Malls peeked out from her breast pocket.

She shook her head. "We got coffee, but I doubt you'd like it."

Carlos gave her a puzzled look. "Why's that?"

"Ain't Mexican." She said nonchalantly as she shrugged her shoulders.

Carlos balked at the casual use of racism. He fought hard not to let his frustration show, but inside, he was seething. This was why he didn't want to come to north Georgia. In his mind, the place was nothing but an antiquated backwater town. Maria had insisted, though, she said the kids needed more nature, and apparently, a week in the mountains was the answer. Carlos hoped the children could avoid a traumatic dose of racism to go with their family vacation.

Swallowing his pride, Carlos said, "Good thing I'm not Mexican then!"

The woman just shrugged and whispered something under her breath. He wasn't sure, but he thought she said something about all Hispanic people looking alike.

The old lady filled a paper cup from the coffee pot behind the counter and set it down in front of Carlos. He quickly dropped a few dollars on the counter and snatched up his coffee, not even bothering with the change. When he got to the door, the woman's smokey voice stopped him.

"You staying on the mountain?" She asked

Carlos nodded.

"Thought so." A sad look came over the old lady's face. "There's one rule on the mountain." The sad look shifted to a stern one. "Watch out for the Reaper."

Carlos' blood ran cold at the ominous statement. "Reaper?" He asked.

The old woman nodded and pointed a shaky finger at the window. "You got kids." She said.

Carlos was surprised it was a statement and not a question, because you couldn't see into the parking lot from her location. Reluctantly, he nodded.

"The Dahlonega Reaper." She said with a tone that implied he should know what she was talking about. With an exhausted look, the old woman reached under the counter and produced a piece of paper that was folded in half. She held it out toward Carlos with one hand and fished a loose cigarette out of her breast pocket with the other. "It's all right here." The woman buried her mouth into the crook of her elbow and unleashed a painful sounding cough. When she pulled her face away from her sleeve, a string of phlegm connected her lips to her shirt. Her cheeks flushed a bright red. She quickly wiped the snot away then shook the paper in the air. "Take it!" She snapped. "You'll need it."

Carlos glanced out the window toward the car. Maria was turned around in her seat, likely yelling at one of the boys for tormenting their little sister. He slumped his shoulders a bit and power-walked across the store.

"Thank you." He said, taking the folded piece of paper.

The woman nodded. She plopped the cigarette between her lips. Producing a lighter from her pocket, she sparked the cigarette. She inhaled deeply, the cherry at the end of the smoke burning a furious red. Exhaling slowly, she blew the smoke into Carlos' face. "If you see someone outside after dark..." her sentence trailed off as her gaze drifted off into space.

Carlos waited a moment to see if the woman was going to come back to the land of the living. When she didn't, he nodded and held up the paper. "Thank you, ma'am." He quickly retreated from the gas station and out the door. The crisp smell of mountain air gave his lungs a reprieve from the cigarette smoke infused air of the gas station.

He set his coffee on the roof of the car and leaned against it. Taking a breath of the clean air, he shook off the strange encounter. With a push on the cover, the lid to the gas pump popped open. Carlos unfolded the piece of paper the strange attendant had given him while the gas pumped into his car.

The page was a simple printout. If Carlos had to guess, he would assume the flyer was created in Microsoft Word and printed on a cheap printer with cheap paper.

It depicted a grainy black and white photo of a child standing in between two trees. The face of the child was completely obscured from view, covered by shadows. Below it, the words "Dahlonega Reaper" were printed in bold type and underlined. His eyes darted around the paper in a rapid fire attempt to read it before the gas tank was full.

"Imitates Loved Ones," and "Don't Let Them Inside," stood out to him immediately. He was starting to read the next sentence when the gas pump clicked. Carlos quickly deposited the paper into his pocket and returned the pump to its home. He dropped into the driver's seat and jammed the key into the ignition.

"Everything good?" Maria asked.

"Never better." He said. The engine roared to life and he threw the vehicle into gear. It jolted forward when he took his foot off the brake. A thud, followed by a swishing sound reminded Carlos that he had left his coffee on the roof. Forcing himself not to look into the mirror at the downed coffee, he pretended not to hear it and pulled out of the gas station.

A few minutes later, Carlos pulled the car into a gravel driveway of a quaint cabin. The rocks crunched under his tires, breaking the otherwise tranquil surroundings. Wooden steps led up to a wrap-around porch with a swing. His eyes drifted to the small pond that peeked out from behind the house. He found himself wondering if there were any fish in the pond, then tried to remember the last time he had gone fishing. Luis' voice interrupted his daydreams.

"Wow!" The boy exclaimed. "This is so cool!" He threw his door open and rushed up the steps, followed closely by Adrian. The two boys made their way over to the porch swing and climbed on.

From behind him, Camila spoke up. "Mommy, can I look at the pond?"

"Of course, sweetie." Maria said. "Just don't get too close to the water."

The girl flashed her mom a big smile then dashed across the yard. She sprinted onto the dock, nearly falling in twice.

Maria looked at Carlos. Her eyes burned with affection. "This is amazing." She said. Leaning toward him, she planted a kiss on his cheek. "Thank you." She whispered in his ear.

"Anything for the family." He said. Together, they climbed out of the car and made their way to the cabin.

The inside of the cabin was even cozier than the pictures on the site had led them to believe. A staircase led to a loft area, and a short hallway went to two bedrooms. The sectional couch wrapped around a fireplace with a flatscreen tv mounted above it.

Maria spun around with her arms outstretched. "This is perfect!" She said through giggles. "I'm going to see what the master bedroom looks like!" With that, she disappeared down the hall and into one of the rooms. She emerged from the room a second later, blushing with embarrassment. "Wrong room!" She turned and disappeared through the next door.

Carlos turned back to the open front door and poked his head out. The sun was setting rapidly behind a wall of tall trees. He wasn't used to how dark it got in the country. Back in the city, the street lights would have kicked on, intermingling with the neon glow of countless signs. Out here, darkness swallowed everything the light couldn't touch.

"Kids!" He shouted. "It's getting dark! Time to come in!"

The patter of feet reverberated across the wooden porch as Luis and Adrian came rushing around the side. The two boys laughed obnoxiously while sprinting past their dad. They jockeyed for position, fighting to be the first inside. Turning his attention away from the boys, Carlos listened for Camila. Nothing. He took a step toward the railing so he could see out over the pond. The dying light made it difficult to see, but he thought he could make out the shape of two figures standing on the dock.

"Camila?" Carlos shouted.

One of the shadowy figures turned their head toward him and waved. The other figure didn't move. An uneasy feeling wormed its way into his stomach. He took the steps two at a time, rushing down to the ground. "Camila?" He repeated. Gravel crunched under his feet. Somewhere in the distance, an owl screeched in the night, announcing the start of its hunt.

Carlos saw the shadowy outline of his daughter turn away from the other figure and run across the dock toward him. The second figure walked behind her at a much slower pace with its head down. Even from this distance, Carlos could tell it was a little girl. Long strands of matted hair hung in front of her as she walked.

"Daddy! I made a friend." Camila said. The light shining through the windows of the cabin hit her. The uneasy feeling in Carlos' stomach faded slightly at the sight of his daughter's smiling face.

She turned and pointed at the shadowy figure behind her. "This is Jennifer." She said.

Carlos waited to see if the girl was going to look up, but she didn't. She continued shuffling toward them, head hung.

"Jennifer got lost, Daddy." Camila said. The young girl bounced on her toes, obviously excited at the prospect of having another little girl to play with while on vacation. "She wants to use our phone to call her parents."

Carlos instinctively patted his pockets. His cell phone wasn't there. He cursed himself for leaving it in the car. Eyeing the little girl, his uneasy feeling returned. Alarm bells went off in his head. Every fiber of his being begged him to kick this creepy little girl into the lake and run back inside. Swallowing the irrational urge, he forced a smile. "Of course she can." Carlos held his hand out for his daughter. "Let's go inside and try the house phone."

Camila reached out to take her father's hand. As soon as their fingers touched, Jennifer's head snapped up. Unnatural yellow eyes stared up at Carlos, reflecting the light from the cabin. Her hair was coated in dried mud, sticks and leaves. The little girl's skin was so white it was nearly translucent.

Sweat broke out across Carlos' forehead despite the cool mountain air. He immediately clasped his fingers around his daughter's hands and yanked her toward him.

"Woah, Dad! You almost knocked me over." Camila exclaimed.

Ignoring her comment, he positioned himself between Jennifer and Camila. The disheveled girl kept her eyes trained on Carlos as he moved.

"Are you ok, Jennifer?" He asked. Carlos did his best to sound confident, but the words came out high-pitched and shaky.

The little girl slowly nodded. She took one exaggerated step toward Carlos. The movement struck him as odd, even though he couldn't seem to place why. Her movements seemed both unsteady and spastic. Those yellow eyes darted quickly back and forth from Carlos to the cabin, then to Camila.

"Well..." Carlos trailed off, knowing what he needed to do but struggling to bring himself to do it. "Let's get you inside." He said in an exasperated tone.

An enormous smile worked its way across Jennifer's face. She nodded again and took an off balance step toward them.

"That." The girl spat the word in a far deeper voice than a little girl should have been able to project. She inhaled deeply. "Would be." Her voice became raspier with every syllable. "Great." The final word sounded painful, as if sandpaper coated her throat.

Carlos slid his hand to his daughter's shoulder and gave her a gentle push toward the cabin. Camila turned and rushed toward the steps. "Jennifer! I can show you my room!" She skipped across the red clay and bounded on the stairs.

Carlos followed behind her at a steady pace, Jennifer walking beside him.

"So, Jennifer..." Carlos said. He watched the girl from the corner of his vision, while she struggled to keep pace with him. She didn't look at him when he spoke. Carlos followed her gaze and realized it was transfixed on Camila's back. "Where are you parents?"

Slowly, Jennifer peeled her eyes off of Camila and turned her head in Carlos' direction. Her smile stretched wide again.

"Burning in hell."

Carlos froze in his spot. He snapped his head toward the little girl. "What did you say?" He asked.

Jennifer stopped and slowly turned to face him. "You heard me, bitch."

The light from the cabin fully illuminated her now and Carlos could see just how... *wrong*, she was. Her features were distorted, like a little girl with melting skin. Carlos took a half step away from her, hands raised.

"Camila! Get in..." Carlos tried to warn his daughter but his sentence was cut short by a sudden shortness of breath and a searing pain in his abdomen. His eyes drifted from his daughter to Jennifer. The girl's horrific visage stared up at him. Her already massive smile stretched wider, opening impossibly large.

Carlos felt a tug in his abdomen. He looked down to see Jennifer's hand embedded up to her elbow in his stomach. Her fingers danced around, massacring his insides, giving him the impression of thousands of spiders crawling through his body. He tried to inhale, desperate to catch his breath. Blood seeped from his open wound. It ran down her arm in thin rivers before dripping from her elbow into a pool on the ground. With a grunt, she forced her arm further into his chest.

He tore his eyes away from the brutal assault on his body in time to see his daughter turn around at the top of the stairs.

Camila's face twisted from one of confusion, to one of shock, and finally, horror. Her shriek filled the air, swirling around Jennifer's haunting laughter. Camila stumbled back into the door, still screaming.

Maria appeared at the door. Her dark hair whipped side to side as she took in the scene before her. She stared through the window and watched as her husband was being murdered.

Carlos felt a tug. There was a suctioning sound, like a drain becoming unclogged. His knees shook for a second, then gave out. He slumped to the ground, gasping for air like a fish out of water.

Jennifer dangled a pink flabby substance over his head. She wiggled it around, teasing him with it. Droplets of blood rained down, coating his face in gore. Falling to her knees, she sunk her teeth into the material in her hand, tearing away a large mouthfull. She leaned in close to Carlos as he continued fighting for a breath of air that never came.

Her lips smacked and bits of chewed tissue fell from her lips. Jennifer leaned in close and whispered in Carlos' ear. "Hard to breathe without lungs." She took another chunk of the lungs into her mouth, gnashing her teeth in front of Carlos. Bits of gore fell from her mouth, piling up on the ground before him. Darkness crept in at the corner of his vision.

The last thing he saw before succumbing to death was the Reaper's yellow eyes.

Maria screamed and threw open the front door. It hit the doorstop and bounced back, nearly smacking her in the face. Wrapping her arms around Camila, she pulled, yanking the girl into the house. Using her foot, she kicked the door closed.

From the loft, the two boys had torn themselves away from their video games long enough to come to the staircase. They leaned over the railing and strained their necks to see what was going on.

Maria's mind kicked into overdrive. She shoved Camila toward the stairs.

"Go upstairs with your brothers!" She shouted.

Camila stared blankly at her mother, appearing to be in a near-catatonic state. Maria snapped her fingers directly in front of Camila's eyes, drawing her to the present.

"Upstairs!" She screamed.

Without bothering to respond, Camila turned and ran up the stairs. Maria listened to the sound of her daughter's footsteps slamming against the wooden steps. The slam of feet against wood ceased, only to be replaced with the sounds of Camila crying and her brother's urgent questions.

Maria looked through the window in the center of the door, where she could see the mockery of a young girl devouring her husband. The little demonic creature buried its hands into Carlos' body, cupping a pool of blood. She brought it to her mouth and drank.

A shiver ran through Maria. She backpedaled away from the door and into the kitchen. Acting on pure adrenaline, she threw open drawers, searching for something to defend her children with. The third drawer gave her what she wanted. Tucked in the back of the drawer was a large carving knife. She pulled out the knife then leaned over the drawer and grabbed her cell phone off the counter.

Turning back toward the door, she dialed 9-1, then stopped. Jennifer was standing in front of the door, staring through the window. Crimson streaks covered her face and hands, decorating her in gore. The little girl raised a blood-soaked hand. She dragged her fingers across the glass, tracing the panes with streaks of red.

The cell phone crashed to the floor. Maria heard the screen shatter but didn't bother looking to confirm. She watched in horror as Jennifer reached out and turned the door handle.

Maria exploded into a sprint, throwing herself against the door as it was opening. Pain radiated through her shoulder from the impact. The door clicked shut, knocking Jennifer back a few feet. Maria's hand fumbled for the deadbolt for a second before finding it. It slid into place with a solid clanking sound.

Jennifer appeared at the glass again. She ran her fingers against the window. Her long nails scratched across the glass like nails on a chalkboard, sending a shiver down Maria's spine. Somewhere behind her, the kids screamed, but Maria blocked it out.

She spun around to find her phone. It was face down a few feet away. She flung herself at it, sliding across the floor. As quickly as she could, she turned it around and pressed the side button to wake up the screen. A white light flashed, revealing a series of cracks stretching across the mangled screen.

Rage boiled up inside Maria's chest. She cocked her head back and screamed. Tossing the useless phone aside, she buried her hands in her hair and screamed again.

"What's wrong, babe?"

Maria's screams fell silent. It was Carlos' voice. She jerked her head in the direction of the voice, only to find a blood-soaked Jennifer staring at her through the window in the door, swaying side to side.

"Did you break your phone again?"

Jennifer's lips moved in perfect harmony with the words, but it was Carlos' voice that rang out through the woods. The cadence and inflection points were off, but it was close enough to make Maria want to open the door.

Slowly, Jennifer turned and walked along the porch, dragging her long nails against the wall and windows. The scratching noise filled the cabin.

Maria pivoted slowly, tracking the sound of the scraping. She watched as Jennifer darted past one of the windows, dragging her fingers along it. The little girl's nails left deep rivets in the glass.

"Open the door, Maria." Carlos' voice rang out.

Maria jerked her head back to the front door. Through the window, she could see Carlos' ruined body laying on the ground in a puddle of his own blood. A sob worked its way into her throat. She forced it back down and crept across the living room to the back door.

This door was little more than a thin sheet of wood. There was no window and it only had a flimsy lock on the handle. Slowly, Maria reached down and clicked the button to lock the door. She pressed her ear to the door and listened.

"Almost had you." She heard a little girl's voice whisper from the other side of the door.

Maria's blood ran cold. She racked her mind for what to do. Her chest tightened and her heartbeat quickened. Her chest rose and fell in ever more rapid succession.

Not now, she begged.

She leaned against the wall, fighting off the impending panic attack. Forcing her eyes open, she stared into the kitchen. Holding her breath in an attempt to control her breathing, she scanned the room, using the various items as focal pints to take her mind off the tightening in her chest. Then her eyes locked on an object hanging on the wall.

There was a phone. Pushing herself off the wall, she propelled herself across the room as quickly as she could.

Maria couldn't remember the last time she had used a landline, but her heart soared when she heard the dial tone. Flipping the phone over, she dialed 9-1-1 and pressed it to her ear.

It rang once, twice, then clicked.

"9-1-1, what's your.."

The line went dead.

"Hello?" She asked. Her lip furled in frustration as she tried again. Nothing. She screamed into the silent cabin and hurled the phone across the room. It impacted the wall and exploded into hundreds of plastic shards.

Maria's chest heaved up and down. There was no way to get help. She smacked herself on the side of the head, willing herself to think of an idea, but none came. Resigning herself to fighting to protect her children, she turned to face the front door.

Luis was standing in front of it. Maria's eyes went wide. She hadn't even heard him come down the stairs. His little hand trembled as he reached out and grabbed the doorknob.

Through the front door's window, Maria could see her husband. He stood in front of the door, grinning maniacally. His head nodded up and down, encouraging the boy.

"Luis! Don't!" She shouted.

But it was too late. Luis pulled the door handle, throwing it open for his father.

Before Maria could react, Carlos exploded through the open doorway, throwing himself onto Luis. The boy screamed when the full weight of his father came down on him.

Maria moved quickly. Sprinting across the cabin, her bare feet smacked against the wood floors, and she threw herself at her husband. She reached him just as he buried his teeth into Luis' neck.

Her shoulder crashed into the pair, sending Carlos sprawling backward. He crashed into an end table. The lamp on top of it rocked precariously on its side before crashing to the floor.

"Mommy?" Luis croaked. His voice came out garbled, like he was trying to speak underwater. Blood seeped from his mouth and the enormous wound in his neck.

"No, no, no." Maria dropped the knife and pressed her hand against Luis' neck, desperately trying to stop the bleeding. "Shhhh. It's going to be ok. Don't try to talk." She said between sobs.

Luis' eyes went wide. The boy coughed, launching blood into his mother's face. He convulsed, every muscle in his body tightening, fighting for life.

Then he went slack.

Maria stared down in disbelief. Being a nurse, she knew what just happened, but she couldn't bring her conscious mind to piece it together. She released a sound that fell somewhere between a shriek and a yell. Pushing herself away from her lifeless son, she crawled backward until she ran into the couch. There she hyperventilated, running her blood stained hands against her face and through her hair, covering herself in a macabre war paint.

"I only wanted the girl."

The thing that looked like Carlos was slowly crawling across the floor. It spoke with the girl's voice, her hauntingly sweet tone dripping off Carlos' lips like poison.

Glancing up, Maria saw her two remaining children leaning over the railing, faces stretched into horrified expressions.

The creature matched her gaze, tilting its head to look up at them. Maria and the monster looked back at each other. There was a frozen second in time where neither reacted. Then, they both exploded into action at the same time.

Carlos scrambled for the stairs.

Maria fell to her belly, stretching to grab the knife. As soon as her fingers wrapped around the handle, she pushed herself up onto all fours and half-crawled, half-ran, as she rushed toward the stairs. She hit the opposite wall, using her momentum to drive her forward. Her eyes shot to the top of the stairs where she saw her husband's legs as he disappeared around the corner into the loft.

A moment later, Camila screamed.

Maria rushed up the stairs. She came around the corner to see Carlos on top of Camila. His hand raised high above his head.

Seemingly from nowhere, Adrian flew through the air. His tiny body landed on Carlos' back, knocking them both off balance. The Carlos thing hissed when it hit the ground, swiping wildly at Adrian.

Maria took the opportunity to lunge forward, driving the knife deep into Carlos' leg. It sliced through his skin like butter, embedding itself in his thigh.

He recoiled, sliding backward on his ass toward the opposite wall. The Carlos thing howled an anguished and angered cry. Its lips furled back to reveal large, sharp teeth. The creature gnashed at its attacker.

Maria flipped onto her back and kicked upward as hard as she could. She connected firmly with the monster's jaw, snapping its head back in a vicious fashion.

Carlos buckled under the onslaught, collapsing to the ground. It scampered away from Maria, holding its injured leg. Black tar oozed from the wound, coating the ground around them.

Maria grabbed Camila by the arm and pulled her away from the monster. She quickly positioned herself between the monster and Camila, then immediately looked for Adrian.

Adrian was standing near the top of the stairs. He was poised to run down the stairs. Tears flowed down his face.

He stared at the monster mimicking his father with confusion.

The beast snapped its head in Adrian's direction and smiled.

Maria's heart smashed against her chest. "Adrian, run!" She screamed.

She launched herself at the monster, stretching her arms to grab it. Her fingers brushed against the sleeve of Carlos' shirt. Unable to hang on, she crashed to the ground. Turning her head, Maria watched helplessly as the Carlos monster crashed into her only remaining son. Together, they fell through the bannister, sending splinters flying in all directions.

The two fell off the edge of the loft, disappearing over the ledge.

Maria's scream mixed with Camila's, each competing for dominance. Maria crawled on all fours to the edge of the loft and gazed over the edge.

The broken remnants of the railing covered the floor below her. Her eyes darted around the darkness, searching for any sign of her son or the monster.

"Adrian?" She yelled. When no reply came, she clambered to her feet.

Maria turned to face her daughter. The girl was curled up at the foot of her bed, rocking gently. Tears streamed down her face and coated her shirt.

Taking a deep breath, Maria tried her best to sound confident for her daughter's sake. "I'm going to get your brother." She wiped away the tears coating Camila's cheek. It wasn't lost on her that she said "brother," as opposed to "brothers." She adjusted her gaze to meet Camila's eyes. "If I'm not back in a couple of minutes, you run out the front door and don't stop running until you get to the neighbor's house. Do you understand?"

Slowly, Camila nodded.

Maria savored what she knew might be her last glimpse of her daughter then rushed down the stairs.

Camila rocked onto all fours and crawled toward the staircase. She listened to the sound of her mother's footsteps receding down the steps. Making it to the edge, she watched her mother hit the ground floor and creep toward the kitchen.

"Adrian?" Maria whispered.

Camila fought the urge to cry out for her brother. She knew she needed to trust her mom to save Adrian, but she felt terrible that she couldn't help. She wiped away more tears from her face.

"Why would Daddy do this?" She whispered to herself.

Camila watched her mom turn toward the hallway that led to the bedrooms. She wrestled with the sobs bubbling up in her throat. Her mother paused and looked up. They locked eyes, then Maria disappeared into the hallway.

Camila stretched her neck to see down the hall, but it was completely obscured from view. She glanced at the front door. It was at the base of the stairs. Camila imagined herself rushing down the stairs and exploding through the door into the cold Georgia air. She stood up and descended the first step. Fearing the repercussions, she paused and listened. She couldn't hear anything. It was as if the world was standing still, the darkness of the cabin swallowing all sound. She took another step and the illusion was shattered.

She heard her mother scream from one of the bedrooms, followed by the sound of shattering glass.

Camila made up her mind and sprinted down the stairs. The sounds of a struggle filled the house. Something crashed into the wall, followed by several grunts. Camila's bare feet smacked against the wooden steps. She ignored the grunts and screams, focusing only on reaching the door. Her hand wrapped around the knob, and without hesitation, she pulled.

The door flew open, smacking against the wall. Camila sprinted through it, not bothering to shut it behind her.

She emerged into the nearly total darkness of the Georgia mountains. The faint glow of a crescent moon gave her enough light to see the porch steps in front of her. She quickly descended them.

She hissed in pain when her bare feet met the rocky ground around the cabin. Ignoring the pain, she pushed forward, trying to remember what direction the nearest neighbor's house was. Camila turned to run, then stopped.

Between her and the woods, stood three small children. They stood completely still, awkward smiles stretched across their tiny faces. Her first instinct was to yell for help, but something stopped her. A knot formed in her stomach when the three children stepped forward in unison.

She spun on her heels to run in the opposite direction, only to see an army of children approaching from the darkness. Her mind raced, she couldn't see a way out. She was about to run toward the back of the house when her mother emerged from the cabin.

Maria leaned against the doorframe, gasping for breath.

"Camila?" She wheezed. Taking a few weak steps forward, she collapsed on the deck. Her hand flailed uselessly, searching for the railing.

Camila sprinted back toward the cabin, bounding up the steps. "Mommy, we have to go. There's more kids!" She shouted. Reaching her mother, she grabbed her mom's arm and pulled.

Maria tried to stand up, but slumped back to the floor. "I don't know if I can run." She said.

Camilla choked back more tears. She glanced over her shoulder at the legion of children emerging from the trees. They moved at a steady pace, seemingly unconcerned with their prey getting away. She grabbed her mother's arm again, but didn't pull.

Black goo gushed from a wound on her mother's thigh and rushed down her leg. Her muscles tensed at the sight of it. Slowly, her eyes drifted up to meet her mother's.

The Maria thing was smiling.

Camila took a step back but the creature lunged out and grabbed her. With incredible strength, it yanked Camilla to the floor and climbed on top of her. The young girl slammed her tiny fists into the monster's chest.

The creature grabbed Camilla by the throat and pinned her head to the porch.

Camilla opened her mouth to scream for help and the monster took the opportunity.

It opened its own mouth and vomited black bile into Camilla's open mouth. The girl's screams were replaced with gags and the sound of splattering liquid as the goo covered the girls face.

Camila's body convulsed into a series of violent seizures. Her arms and legs danced wildly. Her fingers curled and her toes pointed. She convulsed two more times then went slack.

The monster crawled off of Camila. It watched with anticipation, waiting for Camila to react.

After a minute, Camila violently hacked, launching large amounts of the black substance into the air. She rolled onto her side, allowing the goo to slide out of her mouth and onto the porch. Using the sleeve of her shirt, she wiped the mess off her face and sat up. Her head moved from side to side, taking in the sight of the children approaching the cabin and the monster impersonating her mother, She smiled.

The monster smiled back and rose to its feet. It descended the steps into the hoard of smiling children who slowly turned and followed their master into the darkness.

Still smiling, Camila rose to her feet and followed the legion of children toward the next house.

The Man In The Window

Jarvis jolted awake, sweat moistening his forehead. His eyes stretched wide against the abysmal darkness of his room. Blinking hard, they slowly adjusted, allowing him to see the outline of a person standing near his bed. He experienced a brief flash of drowsiness-induced fear before his conscious mind caught up.

"What're you doing, little man?" Jarvis grumbled. He pressed a palm to his eyes, rubbing vigorously to fight away the drowsiness. Rolling onto his side, he inhaled deeply.

"There's a man outside my window." Jordan whimpered. Even in the darkness, Jarvis could see his son trembling.

Jarvis reached out and grabbed the lamp on his bedside table. His fingers fumbled blindly in the dark, searching for the switch. After a moment, his fingers brushed against it, washing the room in a garish light. The illumination blinded him momentarily, and he found himself once again rubbing his eyes and trying to force them to adjust.

When they finally did, he saw Jordan standing before him, tears running down his face. His lip was quivering and he shook violently. A wet spot had formed across the front of his white Spider-Man PJs. Mr. Giggles, his stuffed, purple cat, dangled loosely from his right hand. Its one remaining eye stared back at Jarvis.

Jarvis shook his head, trying to break through the brain fog. "What did you say?" He asked incredulously.

Jordan sniffled and wiped his nose on his sleeve. Jarvis nearly gagged at the sight of a stringy booger clinging to his son's upper lip. "There's a man outside my window." He repeated the statement with a little more confidence this time.

The words punched Jarvis in the chest. His muscles tensed. Pushing himself upright in his bed, he tugged open the top drawer of his bedside table. He yanked the small gun safe out and slammed it onto the bedside table with a loud bang. A red light flashed in the corner of the number pad. His fingers danced across the numbers with practiced ease until the light flashed green. The lid to the safe popped open with a click, revealing the pistol hidden inside. Retrieving the Glock, he cocked the slide back, pausing long enough to ensure there was a round in the chamber. He pulled the pistol tight to his chest and gripped it firmly with both hands.

"Stay here, buddy." Jarvis said as he rested a reassuring hand on his son's shoulder. With a grunt, he rocked himself forward and tiptoed to the door. Jordan let out a soft whimper behind him. Jarvis turned partly, holding out one hand in a "stop" motion. Slowly, he raised his finger to his lips and hushed his son. Jarvis quickly flashed a reassuring smile and then left the room.

The hallway was nearly completely black, save for a few rays of moonlight that fought their way through the sky light and the weak light emanating from his bedroom. The beams of moonlight cast a square ominous glow in the center of the hallway. A shiver ran down Jarvis' spine. He had walked through his house at night for years and never felt alarmed, but for some reason, something felt off. A heaviness hung in the air, making it difficult to breathe. Jarvis continued to creep down the hallway; pistol pulled high to his chest. Years of military training came flooding back with each step, filling him with a renewed sense of confidence.

The door to Jordan's room hung partially ajar, allowing Jarvis to see moonlight pouring in through the window. A jolt of panic ran through him. Those blinds were closed when he put his son to bed. He gripped the door handle with his free hand and took a deep breath. He lowered his eyes, steeling his nerves. With the gun out in front, he exploded into the room. His eyes lead the pistol, quickly scanning the corners of the room for threats before locking onto the window. Holding the gun at the ready, he stared at the window as he cautiously approached it. The curtains were slid apart just as he had suspected. Using a steady heel-to-toe walk, he approached the window, his finger sliding into the trigger guard. His muscles tensed, his finger contracting against the trigger, removing the slack. There was no one there. He expelled a burst of air, fogging up the window. His eyes flicked down to the pistol, where his finger was still pressed firmly against the trigger. He shook his head. That was poor trigger discipline. Releasing the trigger, he kept the gun pointed at the window out of an abundance of caution. The backyard was visible through the window. It was well-lit by the moonlight, allowing Jarvis to see every nook and cranny. Nothing appeared out of place or disturbed. He gazed out over the toys his son hadn't cleaned up and the swing set he had built years ago.

Jarvis lingered at the window for a moment longer before lowering his pistol. He exhaled an exaggerated breath, then retreated from the room. The hallway seemed less intimidating this time. He marched straight through without a second thought until he reached his bedroom door.

When he entered his bedroom, Jordan was still standing in the same spot Jarvis had left him. The little boy had stopped crying but was shifting uncomfortably from leg to leg. His little eyes brightened when he saw his father, only to become transfixed on the pistol in his father's hand. Jarvis quickly slid it behind his back and approached his son.

"There's nobody there, buddy." Jarvis moved past Jordan to the bedside table and returned the pistol to the safe. He closed the lid with a click and waited for the red light to flash, confirming it was locked.

"He was talking to me." Jordan whispered.

Jarvis turned to face his son. He crouched down to the boy's level and rested a reassuring hand on his shoulder. "It was probably just a bad dream, right?" Jarvis suggested. "You remember when you were having those bad dreams about the spiders?" Jarvis shrugged and slid his hand down his son's arm and took his hand. "Same thing." He pushed off of his knee with his free hand, his knees cracking as he stood back up. Jordan wrapped his little fingers around his father's thumb and allowed himself to be led into the bathroom. Jarvis turned the handle for the tub, running his fingers under the water until it warmed up. Once satisfied, he pushed down the plug into the drain. Turning back to his son, he said, "Let's get you cleaned up, kid."

Jordan allowed his dad to strip off his urine-soaked PJs, which Jarvis folded into a towel and set off to the side, then climbed into the tub.

Jordan sat quietly while his dad washed him. Warm water ran over his back and chest. Normally, Jordan would declare himself a "big boy" and snatch the washcloth away from his father, but tonight, he was lost in his own thoughts. Images of the tall silhouette moving around in the yard flashed in his mind like still photos. The duo finished cleaning up and Jarvis hoisted his son out of the bath. He quickly dried him with a towel and wrapped it around the young boy. When they left the bathroom, Jarvis looked around for some clean PJs. "I forgot to grab you some clothes while I was in your room. Go hang out on my bed for a second." He said, kicking himself for being so absentminded.

Jarvis jogged across the room to his bedroom door and quickly turned the corner. He power walked down the hallway, all of the fear and anxiety he had experienced earlier gone. Exploding into Jordan's room, he danced over a few toys that had been left out and retrieved a matching set of Paw Patrol PJs and underwear. Matching Pjs was something Laura always insisted on and after her death, it was a habit the two of them had kept alive. They both knew it was silly, but it made them feel better, like they were helping to keep her memory alive. PJs in hand, he turned to exit the room when something caught his eye. Slowly turning around, his eyes drifted to the window.

On the outside of the window were two enormous hand prints. Jarvis' blood ran cold. Creeping over to the window, Jarvis held his hand up. A chill ran through him at the sudden realization that the imprints of the fingers stretched far longer than his own. It wasn't a bad dream. Jarvis' heart thudded against his chest as he exited the room and sprinted down the hall. His feet smacked loudly against the ground, the sound reverberating off the walls. Exploding through his bedroom door, he saw Jordan sitting on the bed, still wrapped up in a towel. The little boy jumped when his dad burst into the room.

Jarvis scrambled to his son's side and dropped to his knees. They banged painfully into the wood floor. Jarvis hissed away the pain through gritted teeth. "What did the man in the window say to you?" He tried to sound casual about it, as the last thing he wanted to do was alarm his son, but the panic in his voice gave him away.

Jordan shrugged and looked away sheepishly.

"Jordan." Jarvis said sternly. "What did the man say?"

"He asked me to open the window." Jordan whispered. Another round of tears welled up in his eyes. He released a soft sniffle. "He said he could take me somewhere fun."

Jordan lifted his eyes to meet his father's gaze. "But he said you couldn't come."

Jarvis jumped up and grabbed his cell phone off the nightstand. He quickly punched in 9-1-1 and pressed the green call button at the bottom of the screen.

The phone rang once. Twice. Then, a serious-sounding lady answered. "9-1-1, do you need fire, medical, or police?"

Jarvis froze up. The momentary thought of hanging up drifted through his mind. This was silly; there was nobody there and if there had been, they were long gone by now. He glanced down at his teary-eyed son and shook his head. Unsure what to say, he answered, "Ugh, police, I think."

"Ok, sir. And what is the nature of your emergency?" This woman was all business. She spoke with the calm demeanor of someone who had done this a thousand times before.

Jarvis turned his back to his son to prevent him from hearing the conversation. "I think someone tried to break into my house." He whispered.

"Are they in the house now?"

Jarvis looked around as if a man was going to miraculously appear out of thin air. "No, ma'am. I don't think so." Jarvis paused, unsure how much information he should give them. "He was outside my son's window."

She spent the next minute or so collecting Jarvis' personal information and assured him an officer would be there shortly. Jarvis ended the call and tossed the phone onto the bed. Turning around to face his son, he realized the boy was still not dressed. "I'm sorry, buddy. Daddy is going to have a police officer come over just to be safe. Ok?" Jordan nodded.

"Like Chase?" Jordan asked, pointing at the police dog on his PJs.

Jarvis cracked a smile. He ruffled his son's hair and said, "Yeah, buddy, Just like Chase."

Jarvis helped his son into his PJs and the two of them huddled together in Jarvis' bed until the doorbell rang. Tentatively, the two made their way into the living room. Before opening the door, Jarvis peeked through the peep-hole. A uniformed police officer stood on the porch. Jarvis motioned to the couch and Jordan jumped onto it; then Jarvis opened the front door.

The officer was a chubby man with a comically large mustache. The officer quickly informed Jarvis that he had done a sweep of the property and saw nobody out there. His mustache whiskers blew in and out like a cartoon with every breath. Trying to put Jarvis at ease, the officer ran down a short list of possibilities, most of which Jarvis had already considered. The officer seemed convinced it was either a bad dream or teenagers pulling a prank. According to the officer, there were no hand prints on the window or any footsteps in the mud around the house. Jarvis listened patiently until the officer finished, leaving him completely unsatisfied with this man's dedication to serving and protecting.

"Y'all just call back if you see or hear anything else." The officer instructed, then exited the house. Jarvis waited a moment, then slid the deadbolt closed behind him. Pressing his forehead against the cool metal door, he fought off the urge to call the officer back and request he perform another sweep of the house.

Turning to his son, he forced a smile. "See, buddy? It's all clear!" He reached down and scooped Jordan up. "Airplane?" He asked.

"Yes, please!" Jordan exclaimed, then held out his arms to his sides like wings. Jarvis made a series of airplane noises as they ran back to his bedroom. "Coming in for a landing!" Jarvis said before gently setting Jordan down on the bed. Jordan giggled like it was the funniest thing he had ever experienced, despite the fact that they did this same routine several times a week. Jarvis peeled the covers back and tucked the boy in.

"Daddy?" Jordan asked.

"Yeah, buddy?" Jarvis moved around to his side of the bed and pulled the covers back.

"Why did you call the police if it was all a dream?"

Jarvis stopped what he was doing. He stared at his young son in amazement. "You're too smart for your own good, you know that?" He asked incredulously. Sliding into the bed next to Jordan, he tried to think of an answer that was both truthful and wouldn't frighten his son any further. "I guess I just wanted to make extra, super-duper sure that it wasn't real."

Jordan looked up and tapped his chin like he was concentrating on a particularly hard math equation. "I guess that makes sense." He stated, then shrugged. "Alright. Goodnight, Dad!" Jordan leaned forward and kissed his dad on the forehead and closed his eyes.

"Goodnight, kiddo." Jarvis said, flicking off the bedside lamp and rolling to face his son. It was completely dark in the room except for the little bit of moonlight bleeding in through the window. Within a few minutes, he was fast asleep.

A quiet noise woke Jarvis up a short time later. Rubbing at his eyes, he strained his ears for the sound. It sounded like Jordan was whispering to him. The squeak of his young voice was hard to decipher. Jarvis sighed heavily, the poor boy was probably scared again. He rolled over to face his son and stretched his hand out, only for it to fall flat on the pillow. Panic surged in his chest. His hand flew frantically around the bed, searching for any sign of his son.

Jordan was not on the bed.

Jarvis flipped over, his hand instinctively going for the lamp. His fingers found the switch and he began to flip it but stopped short.

Jordan was standing in front of the window. The young boy's small frame was silhouetted against the moonlight now pouring through the open window. He was staring almost straight up, as if looking at someone much taller than himself. In the darkness, Jarvis could tell the boy's mouth was moving at a rapid pace, his whispers growing faster and more incoherent with every second.

Jarvis thought he could make out a few words here and there. He held his breath, trying to understand his son's rambling.

"Faceless."

"Tall."

"My daddy."

"Kill."

The ramblings continued with only momentary pauses between whispers. It carried the cadence of an excited conversation.

Hearing enough, he set his fingers on the switch for the bedside lamp. Just as he was about to pull the switch, he heard someone say, "awake."

The voice was not his son's. It was deeper, more guttural. It echoed loudly around the room as if it was coming from all directions at once. Almost against his will, his eyes left his son, scanning the darkness for the source of this inhuman voice. When nothing materialized, he glanced back at his son.

Jordan was facing him now.

The boy's eyes were stretched open wide. His normally brownish-green eyes flooded with black. His mouth opened into a mockery of a scream. Jordan's arm shot straight out, elbow locked. The index finger on his right hand pointed directly at Jarvis.

Jarvis braced himself for a shout or a scream, but none came. He flicked on the light. In that briefest of moments, before the light wrestled away the darkness, Jarvis could have sworn he saw the outline of an impossibly tall man standing behind his son, his unnaturally long, slender fingers wrapped around the boy's throat. Before Jarvis' mind could fully register what he saw, he blinked and the apparition vanished.

Jordan's face went slack and the boy slumped to the floor, unconscious.

Without hesitation, Jarvis propelled himself out of bed and rushed to his son's side. The boy's light brown skin was now a ghastly hue. His fingers trembled and convulsed, sending a pang of fear into Jarvis' chest. Jarvis slid his arm under his son's head and lifted him off the floor.

"Jordan? Jordan!" He screamed. He shook the boy, gently at first, then harder as his desperation won out. Slowly, Jordan opened his eyes.

"Daddy?" Jordan whimpered.

"Yeah, buddy. It's me." He pressed his son's face into his chest and squeezed him tightly. "You scared me." Jarvis said. Tears poured down his face, drenching his son's hair.

"I think I had another bad dream." Jordan cried softly. "The faceless man asked to come in." He started crying even harder. "He said he wanted to wear your face." The crying turned into inconsolable sobbing. "He said he wanted to be my daddy now!" Jordan squirmed against his father's grip. "I don't want him to be my daddy!"

Jarvis squeezed his son and tried to shush him. Jordan's cries filled the room as Jarvis tried desperately to soothe his terrified boy.

"I didn't want to let him in, Daddy. I promise I didn't!"

"It's ok, little man. It was just a bad dream."

"Why did I let him in?" Jordan cried.

Goosebumps broke out across Jarvis' back and arms. The uneasy feeling of being watched crept over him. "What do you mean?" Jarvis asked, hesitantly.

"I opened the window. It was just a little bit, but he got in!"

Panic tore through Jarvis' system. His heart thudded painfully against the walls of his chest. Jarvis' head snapped toward the window.

It was open.

It was only a few inches of space, but the sight sent an icy bolt of fear down Jarvis' spine. Ice flooded his veins. He looked down at his son, who had his eyes clenched shut.

"Jordan, I need you to tell me the truth. Was there a man at the window?" He took his son's face into his hands. "Son, I promise I won't be mad."

Jordan shook his head. His sobbing subsided and he leaned in close to his dad's ear.

"He's in the house." The boy whispered.

As soon as the words left the child's mouth, a cold gust of air swept in from the opposite side of the room, causing Jarvis to whip his head around. There was an unnatural darkness within the shadows. It loomed large, its blurry mass darker than the shadows around it. It grew larger and quickly took shape.

An incredibly tall man with unnaturally long extremities came into view. Long, thin fingers dangled from bony hands. It stepped out of the shadows and into the light.

Its face was a wall of pale, white skin. This creature had no discernible characteristics. No nose, no eyes, and worst of all, no mouth. The monstrosity lingered there momentarily, gently swaying side to side like it was trying to keep its balance. Then, without warning, it sprinted forward. Before Jarvis could react, it leaped toward him and Jordan.

Thinking only of his son, Jarvis pushed the young boy out of the way. His small frame skidded against the floor before crashing into the bedside table, knocking over the lamp. It rolled to the edge of the table before falling to the ground, shattering into pieces. The room plummeted into near total darkness.

"Run, Jordan!" Jarvis commanded.

Jordan didn't move. The boy curled into a ball at the base of the bedside table, staring at the monstrosity crawling over his father. It moved like a spider, crawling on all fours. Its lanky limbs hoisting it high off the ground. The monster's fingers felt around, blindly searching for Jarvis' arms.

Jarvis tried to kick. He squirmed and tried to roll over, but it was no use. The creature's elongated hands wrapped around his wrist. The weight of the monster pinned him to the floor as it slowly lowered its featureless face toward his own.

Jarvis screamed as loud as he could. "Jordan! Please! Run!"

The creature's suffocating weight pushed down onto him, expelling the air from his lungs. He gasped for breath as the creature's face pressed against his own. Searing pain tore through his cheek as his skin melted away. The burning spread across his head like a river of lava. Blisters bubbled to the surface of his skin before popping under the unrelenting heat. The skin peeled away, revealing the sinew hidden below. Jarvis bucked with all his might, desperately trying to save himself from the burning. A sickening squelch filled his ears as his left eye went dark. His one remaining eye flew open.

He saw Jordan sitting there, utter horror stretched across the small child's face.

Jarvis desperately reached out for something to grab onto but came up short. The burning seemed to dissipate.

The creature splayed itself out, lowering ever deeper onto its prey. Jarvis released one last cry for help before succumbing to the encroaching darkness of unconsciousness.

Petrified, Jordan could do nothing but watch as the faceless man melded with his father, absorbing his characteristics. After a few more moments, the faceless man and his father were indistinguishable from one another, instead forming an analogous blob. They continued morphing and melting into one another until his father's screams faded to a whisper. Jordan squeezed his eyes shut and pressed his hands over his ears. He screamed in horror and pain, begging for the faceless man to stop.

He continued blocking out the world until he felt a gentle pull on his hand. Slowly, he allowed whoever it was to peel his hands away. Opening his eyes, he saw his father.

A smile stretched across Jordan's face and he propelled himself forward, wrapping his arms around his father's waist. The boy squeezed as tightly as he could, afraid to let his father go again. His father didn't return the hug.

Daring to release his father, Jordan looked up into his eyes. He thought his dad seemed taller than normal and couldn't seem to make sense of it, but his father's features seemed distorted. Long, bony fingers reached out and took Jordan's hand. Without a word, his father guided him to the window. The window slid open as they approached.

His much taller father stepped through the open window before lifting him over the wall and setting him down in the grass. Sticky mud wiggled between his toes and Jordan shivered in the night air. The taller daddy took a step forward, pulling him along.

Together, they walked into the darkness of the forest behind the house.

The Valley of Missing Children

Regan eased the car around the bend and into the parking lot of a rundown gas station. A single overhead light did its best to illuminate the area through its dirt-coated bulb. The building seemed to lean to one side. Regan thought the building looked as if it might collapse at any minute. A cheap coat of white paint peeled away in places to reveal the rotting wood beneath it. Rust and grime coated every surface. The brakes of her car screamed when she stopped in front of the pump. She shook her head. Brian had promised to replace the brakes weeks ago, but then again, he had promised a lot of things. With the thought of Brian, her eyes began to water.

Wiping away a lone tear at the corner of her eye, Regan glanced in the rearview mirror. Charlie was fast asleep. He leaned against the window with his blue blanket tucked in under his chin. Mr. Rafe, Charlie's favorite stuffed giraffe, peeked out from under the blanket. At some point during the drive, he must have kicked off his shoes because his little toes stuck out from under the blanket. Her eyes flickered from Charlie to herself then away again. She couldn't stand to look at her own sickly appearance. Leaning her head against the headrest, she closed her eyes. The action brought immediate relief to the bloodshot orbs. She inhaled deeply, fighting against the overwhelming fatigue plaguing her whole body.

She had nearly drifted off to sleep when she heard a gentle tap on her window.

"You ok, Ma'am?" A husky voice asked.

Regan bolted upright. A thick fog had settled over her mind, making it difficult to determine where the voice had come from. Her eyes darted back and forth, searching for the source of the noise. They landed on the chubby, middle-aged man standing outside her window. The bottom of his belly poked out from beneath a sweat-stained white shirt.

A pang of fear ripped through her chest. Her breaths grew rapid and shallow. When she looked his way, he stepped away from her window with his hands up. His kind blue eyes didn't match his scruffy appearance, giving Regan a sense of relief. He cracked a smile, revealing a row of smoke-stained teeth and dashing away the brief sense of relief..

"Didn't mean to startle you, ma'am." He pointed to his name tag. "I'm Doug."

Regan looked at the name tag, then back at the building. A decrepit sign with faded words hung in the windows. It read, "Doug's Gas and Service." Regan released a sigh of relief. She glanced back at Charlie to make sure he was still asleep, then pushed open her door.

"I'm really sorry about that." She said. Out of habit, Regan lowered her eyes to avoid Doug's gaze. "I was just resting my eyes for a second." Breaking her own rules, she chanced a glance at Doug's face. He was staring at the purple bruises that pockmarked her arms. She cursed herself for taking off her sweater.

After a prolonged moment of silence, Doug waved his hand dismissively. "That's quite alright, Ma'am." He pointed to the gas pump. "Need a hand pumping your gas?"

Regan shook her head. "No, thank you. I can do it." She tried to sound confident, but the words came out shaky and unsure.

Doug shrugged. "No problem! Just head on inside when you're done." He patted the gas pump. "Unfortunately, I don't have any fancy card readers in this thing."

He flashed her another smile, whistling a tune as he walked away.

She watched him walk back into the store and disappear from view before exhaling. Her chest quivered. She clenched her eyes together, trying to remember what the social worker had said about panic attacks. Regan took a few steps back until her back brushed up against the gas pump. Following the social worker's guidance, she leaned her head back and inhaled deeply. Her fingers crawled across the gas pump until she found a rough patch. The spot felt dirty, but she didn't care. She exhaled, focusing on the feeling in her fingers. The jagged edges of the worn-down gas pump threatened to tear the skin on the tips of her fingers, but it also took her mind away from her fear. The tightening grip on her chest loosened and her heart rate slowed. Inhale. The knot in her stomach untwisted. Exhale. She opened her eyes. Shaking her head, Regan threw open the gas cap of her car and jammed the gas pump inside. She watched the number tick up as she filled her car. A feeling of self-loathing crept its way into her mind. She knew she needed to deal with her trauma. There was no way she could get through life while having a panic attack every time she spoke to a man, but right now, she just needed to make it through this drive. When the handle clicked, she pulled it out of her car and returned it to the pump.

A quick glance into the back seat of the car told her Charlie was still asleep. Her son had twisted in his seat and was now hugging the stuffed giraffe. Satisfied that he wouldn't wake up, she scurried across the parking lot and entered the store.

The store was just as dingy on the inside as it was on the outside. A hint of mildew hung in the air. It wasn't powerful enough to make it unbearable; instead, it was more of a minor discomfort. A single shelving unit housed various snacks and led down to a one-door cooler that was filled almost completely with beer. On the opposite wall was a roller grill for hotdogs. The machine was covered in cobwebs and a layer of aged grease. Regan smiled at the coffee machine beside the old roller grill. It hummed as it brewed a fresh pot.

"You looked like you needed a cup." Doug's voice boomed out from behind the counter. Regan's hand flew to her chest and she swallowed hard.

"Yes." She croaked out quietly. Clearing her throat, she tried again. "Yes, thank you." She moved along the single shelf, grabbing a couple of bags of chips and a roll of chocolate chip cookies for Charlie. She reached the cooler and retrieved an apple juice. The sight of a Budweiser can nearly sent her into another panic attack. Quickly tearing her eyes away, she rushed back to the counter and deposited the snacks. Doug had moved from around the counter and filled up a large styrofoam cup from the coffee pot.

"I don't have any creamer or nothing." He glanced down at the black coffee in his hand. "I hope that's alright."

Regan put on her best smile. She hated black coffee, but right now, she was desperate. "That's perfect." She lied.

Doug smiled and set the cup on the counter next to the other items. He rang up the chips and cookies before pointing at the coffee. "This one is on the house."

Regan smiled. "Thank you. " She whispered while fishing a few bills from her wallet and handing them over. A picture of her in an Arizona State softball uniform fell out her wallet. Regan quickly grabbed it off the counter and tucked it back into her wallet.

"You played softball?" Doug asked.

Regan smiled politely and nodded. "Not for a long time."

The man nodded. "I heard that. I played football myself. Was all county."

She nodded while waiting for him to make her change. Regan looked out the window toward her car. Charlie was still sound asleep with his head against the window.

Turning her attention back to Doug, Regan tried to work up the courage to ask him for directions.

Doug either read her mind, or was used to people needing directions while passing by his shop, because he brought it up before she managed to muster the courage.

"You wouldn't happen to be lost would ya?"

Regan nodded slowly. "I'm trying to get to Pittsburgh." She motioned toward the car. "My GPS is pretty much useless out here."

Doug rubbed his chin. "Well, there's two good ways to get to the steel city from here." He reached under the counter and retrieved a map. Laying it out across the counter, he pointed to a road. "There's the safe way." He paused and moved his finger to another road. "Then there's the fast way."

"Is the fast way..."

Doug cut her off. "It's dangerous. Highway Fifteen cuts through the valley." He moved his hand in a circle on the map. "There's no lights, no guardrails, and no people. I'd recommend taking the safer road."

Regan weighed her options. The drive from Albuquerque had been grueling and she had already been on the road for over twenty hours. With only a small nap somewhere outside of Indianapolis, she wasn't sure how much longer she could drive for.

"I just need to get there as quickly as possible."

Doug nodded. "Alright. Through the valley then." He pointed to the road again, then to the window. "You'll take this road right here for about a mile. You'll see a sign for Highway Fifteen. The turn-off is about a mile after that. You'll see a sign that says, 'Beware the valley of missing children,' it's painted in big red letters. That's where you turn."

A shiver ran up Regan's spine. Her eyes instantly flew toward the window. Charlie was still asleep in his seat. Turning her attention back to Doug, she asked, "Why do they call it that?"

Doug shrugged. "Superstition. Lot of people have gone missing out that way." He waved it off. "Like I said, it's local superstition." He traced the map with his finger. You'll take it for about twenty miles. Then," he tapped a spot on the map. "You'll hit Highway 30 and ride that all the way to Pittsburgh."

Regan gave Doug her sweetest smile. She considered asking him about the other route but elected not to. There was no more time and no more money. Her parents would take care of her and Charlie, all she had to do was get there.

Regan thanked the kind gas station manager and gathered her things. She deposited her goods into the car and fired up the old shitbox. The motor of her 95' Camry whined momentarily before roaring to life. Waving through her window at Doug, she eased the car back onto the road and gassed it. This close to Pittsburgh, a sense of freedom washed over her. She considered cracking her window and allowing the cool Pennsylvania air to blow through her hair, but stopped when Charlie pivoted in his seat. His blanket slid down his body, revealing the blue cast on his arm. The sight of the shoulder-height cast sent a pang of guilt through her heart, causing any feeling of relief or freedom to fade. Regan kicked herself for not leaving sooner and found herself once again fighting the urge to cry. It surprised her that she could still generate tears. Shaking them away, she steeled her mind for the last leg of their journey. The needle on the speedometer climbed as she pressed harder on the peddle. She willed for the journey to end and for the warmth of her childhood bed. They were nearly there.

She blew past the first sign for Highway fifteen, doing twenty above the speed limit. "Just get to Pittsburgh." She repeated the mantra over and over in her head. If they could just get there, they could start life over. They could start the healing process. She glanced down at her own bruised and battered body. Choking back a sob, she swore to herself that she would never let another man hit her as long as she lived.

A large wooden sign appeared on the side of the road. It rose out of the darkness like an apparition. In red hand-painted letters, it read precisely as Doug had said it would.

"Beware The Valley Of Missing Children"

Regan's stomach twisted into a knot. She glanced back at her sleeping son and his cast. For a second, she considered turning around and asking Doug for directions to the safer route. The ominous sounding valley was getting to her, goosebumps breaking out across her skin. She repeated her mantra out loud this time.

"Just get to Pittsburgh." Regan whispered. The words sounded weak, even to her. Inhaling sharply and tightening her grip on the steering wheel, she tried again. "Just get to Pittsburgh." She said through gritted teeth. A smile teased at the edge of her mouth. Maybe there was a little fight left in her after all.

With that, she threw on her blinker and turned down the exit. Her headlights illuminated the road directly in front of her. All around her car, darkness and shadows danced, obscuring their surroundings. The vague shape of trees stretching into the black sky zipped past the windows. The yellow paint on the road demarcating the lanes faded until the road morphed into a single lane.

The heaviness in her eyelids bore down on her, beckoning her to rest her eyes for a moment. Regan tried to rub the drowsiness away one eye at a time, careful not to take both eyes off the road at the same time.

Just a few more hours, she thought to herself.

Regan shook her head and grabbed the cup of coffee from the cup holder. The bitter aroma filled the car and grew stronger as she brought it to her lips. Warmth radiated from the cup, feeling good in her hand. Just as she was about to take a sip, the car hit a steep incline in the road. The sudden impact jolted the vehicle and sent a splash of scalding hot coffee onto her lap. Brown liquid ran down her legs, the searing pain burning a path across her thighs.

"Fuck!" She shouted. As soon as the expletive left her mouth, her eyes flew to the rearview mirror. Charlie stirred slightly, then resumed his rhythmic breathing. Regan sighed. The last thing she needed was a cranky six-year-old who wouldn't go back to sleep.

The stinging sensation of the hot coffee seeping through her pants pulled her mind back to the issue at hand. She returned the coffee to the cup holder and leaned across the center console. Pulling her eyes from the road, she fidgeted with the handle of the glovebox, but it didn't fall open. Cursing under her breath, she remembered that the glovebox often got stuck. She gripped the handle tightly, and

she tugged hard. There was a loud click and the glovebox
fell open.

She brought her eyes back up to the road before returning to her hunt for napkins. Feeling around blindly, she
pushed aside an owner's manual and her car's registration.
Her hand continued dancing across random objects in the
glovebox, unable to find anything to clean herself up with.

"Come the fuck on." She muttered under her breath.
Peeling her eyes away from the road, she gazed into the
glovebox. The corner of a brown napkin peeked out from
underneath the thick owner's manual.

"Gotcha." She said triumphantly.

Leaning a bit further, she grasped the corner of the napkin and tugged. It came away easily. Regan sat back up and
returned her eyes to the road.

Her headlights caught the outline of a person standing
in the middle of the road, directly in front of her. The next
few seconds played out in her mind in slow motion. The
shadowy apparition came into full view. A blonde girl with
a yellow dress twirled in the road, just feet from the front
of her car.

Regan reacted more out of instinct than coherent
thought. Her foot shifted from the gas to the brake and
slammed the pedal to the floor. The tires locked up, their
screech filling the night air. Her subconscious mind real-

ized that she wouldn't stop in time before Regan was fully aware of it. Jerking the wheel to the right, her foot slid off the brakes. The car veered hard to the right, missing the little girl by inches. Regan saw the blur of her yellow dress out of the driver's side window as the car rifled past her.

The front tires of the car left the pavement. They hit the gravel on the side, jostling the car's occupants harder. Behind her, Charlie screamed, now very awake.

"Mommy!" His panicked cry shattered her heart into a million pieces.

She tried to slam on the brake again, but the car hit an embankment, lifting the front tires off the ground. Regan experienced a moment of peaceful weightlessness as the car soared off the edge of a cliff. That momentary reprieve quickly washed away. The car plummeted toward the Earth. Coffee and snacks went flying through the air. Regan squeezed her eyes shut, fighting the nausea broiling in her stomach. A feeling of helplessness overcame her. She knew all she could do was hope. Hope that she and her son would survive this wreck. Hope that someone would rescue them.

Hope and wait.

The car listed to one side, followed by a bone-jarring impact. The front of the vehicle hit a massive outcropping of rocks, sending it tumbling end over end. Regan's head snapped forward, meeting the exploding airbags at full force. Her seatbelt tightened, sending pain exploding through her body.

A scream filled the car. Regan couldn't be sure if it came from her, Charlie, or both, but it filled the air all around her. The nose of her car pitched forward one more time. An enormous tree rushed up to meet her, filling Regan's view through the windshield. A second later, the car impacted the ground and everything went black.

A faint crackling filled the air. It reminded Regan of so many bonfires she attended as a teenager. Distantly, Regan could smell something cooking. She thought it smelled like burnt plastic. She tried to open her eyes, but couldn't see anything. Her heart thundered against her chest as her hands flew to her face. They smeared warm liquid around as she fought to clear her face. She managed to open her right eye and her heart skipped a beat. The car was upside down, leaving them hanging, her seat belt digging into her skin. Black smoke bellowed into the cab from every crack and crevice around her. From outside the wreckage, the crackling noise grew louder. The cloud of noxious fumes around her thickened, burning her eyes and nose.

"Charlie?" She croaked. Smoke filled her lungs, sending her into a coughing fit. Fighting through coughs that racked her whole body, she tried to call for her son. "Charlie?" She screamed again. No answer. Regan tried to twist in her seat but couldn't turn enough to see behind her.

The orange glow of flames grew brighter all around her. Embers peeked out from the floor and behind the dashboard. Blood from her busted lip flowed across her face, filling her eyes. She fumbled blindly with her seatbelt. Her hands trembled as they searched. As soon as her fingers found the button, she clicked it. The belt went slack, and she crashed to the ground, bits of broken glass stabbing into her skin.

Wincing from the broken shards digging into her palms, She whirled around. "Charlie?" She screamed.

Charlie's car seat was empty, his restraints undone. Regan's mouth flew open. Her mind raced through the possibilities. She tried to scream again, but the smoke was too thick. She coughed hard, sending a new wave of pain through her body. Her eyes darted around the interior of her ruined car, searching desperately for her missing boy. A crippling pain radiated through her left leg. Looking back, the flames were burning their way through the dashboard and licking at her skin. She bit into the palm of her hand to keep from screaming. Sweat broke out across her body, drenching her clothes. The inside of her car trapped the heat, turning the vehicle into an oven.

Confident Charlie was no longer in the car, Regan rolled onto her back and slid under the front seats. Bits of broken glass tore at her shirt and embedded themselves into her skin. Regan could feel her blood rushing to the surface and soaking the tattered remnants of her shirt. Gritting her teeth, she pushed hard, slithering like a snake, away from the fire. Once she made it under the seats, she rolled onto her stomach, still ignoring the pain spreading across her body and crawled out of the shattered rear window.

Emerging from the burning wreckage, she gasped for clean air. Her lungs seized, forcing her to fight for each breath. Frigid night air embraced her, washing away the burning sensation spreading across her body. She clenched her eyes shut and forced herself to take a deep breath of clean air, only to violently hack again.

"Char-" She fought against the tightening of her chest. "Charlie?" She screamed.

The whoosh of flames answered her as they engulfed the car behind her. Regan forced herself onto her hands and knees and crawled away from the inferno. Thick mud clung to her clothes and coated her various cuts in dirt.

She continued crawling until she reached a tree. Leaning up against it, Regan wiped blood from her face, replacing it with a thick layer of grime. Her eyes darted around wildly, searching for her missing son. Charlie was nowhere to be seen. The images of the road sign flashed in her mind. "Beware The Valley Of Missing Children."

The flipped car leaned against a tree, flames rising out of it and reaching for the sky. The fire bathed the clearing in an orangish hue. All around her, shadows danced in and out of trees and bushes.

"Charlie!" She screamed again. The fear of dying in a ball of flames had vanished, only to be replaced with the fear of not finding her son. Regan opened her mouth to scream again when she noticed movement out of the corner of her eye.

A long, gray hand, wrapped around the trunk of a tree. Slender fingers unfurled and tapped against the trunk. Regan's mouth fell open and her eyes stretched wide. She started to scream but stopped short. The hand darted back into the shadows, disappearing behind the tree. Regan blinked hard then rubbed her eyes. She rubbed her face. Did she really just see that? She squeezed her eyes shut and shook her head. When she opened them, there was nothing there.

"Mommy!"

Regan jerked her head. Her heart soared at the sound of her little boy's voice, but dropped as the realization that he was screaming set in. Charlie's scream sounded panicked and scared. Without any more hesitation, she pushed herself to her feet and stumbled in the direction of the voice.

"Mommy! Help!" Charlie's voice sounded further now.

"Charlie! I'm coming!" She screamed. Leaning forward, Regan pumped her legs as hard as she could, sprinting across the field and into the opposite trees. Branches scratched against her face, and roots threatened to trip her, but Regan pushed herself to run faster.

"Mommy!" Charlie's cries were faint now. The natural rustle of the forest drowned out the echoes of his screams as they faded into the forest. Regan racked her brain. There was no possible way the little boy was outrunning her, especially not with a broken arm. She sprinted through the trees, not even bothering to shield herself from the onslaught of nature tearing at her flesh. She ran until she couldn't possibly run anymore and her lungs threatened to explode. Just as she was about to give up, her foot caught a root protruding out of the ground. The sudden impact sent her tumbling forward. Her chest slammed against the ground, expelling the air from her lungs. Unable to stop her momentum, she slid face-first down an embankment and into a ditch.

Regan lay flat in the ditch with her head to the side, sucking in air. She inhaled deeply, trying to build up the strength to press on. Every inch of her body screamed in pain, and the cut on her lip kept reopening. The muck at the bottom of the ditch soaked into her already ruined clothes. She shivered, the cold of the forest seeping into her bones. The little voice inside her head begged her to give up. It encouraged her to roll onto her side and curl up in the fetal position and cry. Charlie's panicked screams echoed in her mind, drowning out the sense of doubt. Doing a push-up, Regan pulled her head from the ground, the wet forest floor making a slurping sound when she did. Thick mud squeezed between her fingers. An ungodly stench wafted up from the mud. Regan wrinkled her nose, trying to figure out what was causing the smell. It reminded her of the time the refrigerator died and all of their food spoiled.

Regan rolled onto her ass, ignoring the stench and the wetness spreading across her bottom. Looking around, she noticed something strange sticking out of the ground next to her. A jagged white rock protruded from the dirt. She knew she needed to press on and find her child, but something about the rock didn't feel right. Everything else around her was covered in mud and dirt, while this was pristine. It stuck out like a sore thumb and it beckoned her to investigate.

Her hand trembled as she reached out toward it. She wrapped her fingers around the rough material and pulled. It came loose from the ground with a plopping sound.

Regan turned her hand over to examine the object. Recognition dawned across her face and she screamed. She dropped the object and scrambled away from it, dragging herself through the mud. Hard, jagged objects jabbed into her hands and legs. For the first time, she noticed the white rocks all around her. Only, they weren't rocks. Looking for a way out of the macabre hole, her eyes locked onto a human skull. Another scream lodged in her throat as she stared at the bones in disbelief.

Regan clambered to her feet and threw herself onto the embankment. Her fingers dug into the thick mud. It splashed up her arms and covered most of her body. With massive fear-induced pulls, she clawed her way out of the ditch. Gasping for air, she reached the top and risked a look back into the ditch.

Human bones protruded from the mud in different angles. The brown of the mud intermingled with decaying corpses and blood gave it a reddish tint. Flies buzzed around the cesspool, gorging themselves on remains. Nausea broiled in Regan's stomach and exploded upward before she could attempt to stifle it. She turned and vomited into a bush next to her.

Wiping vomit from her lips, Regan inhaled deeply. Turning away from the gory scene behind her, she tried shouting for her son again.

"Charlie!" She yelled as loud as she could. Cupping her mouth with both hands, she yelled again. "Charlie!"

Regan closed her eyes, and listened. The response she received sent goosebumps rippling up her arms.

Her own voice screamed back at her.

Or, it was nearly the same. The pitch and tone were right, but it seemed somehow devoid of emotion. Her voice trembled when she spoke again.

"Ch... Charlie?" She stammered.

"I'm right here, Mommy."

Regan jerked her head to the right to see her son standing only a few feet away from her. Relief flooded her body. She took a step toward him, ready to scoop the boy up into her arms. Then she noticed his cast was gone. Regan froze.

Charlie pitched his head to the side. His eyes bore into Regan's. "What's wrong, Mommy?"

It sounded so much like her son that Regan wanted to launch herself at the boy and wrap him into a hug. But she couldn't shake the feeling that something wasn't right.

"Mommy, I'm scared." He said again. The masquerade slipped, and Regan heard it. There was the faintest hint of a deeper voice just behind the words.

Regan took a step back, fully aware that the ditch was only a few feet behind her.

"Where's your cast?" Regan asked sternly.

Charlie looked down at the arm and shook his head. His head jerked up and he locked eyes with Regan again. The blue in Charlie's eyes melted away, his pupils growing impossibly large until they encompassed the entirety of each eye. Regan could do nothing but stare into the obsidian orbs.

The creature tilted its head and smiled. It's teeth morphed into razor-like fangs. "I thought I had you." The monster said in a flat, monotone voice. The visage of her son melted away, replaced by wrinkling, gray skin. Tilting its head the other way, the Charlie thing winked. "You should run." It said.

Regan pivoted to her left and ran. She pumped her arms and legs as fast as she could. Her feet landed dangerously close to the edge of the ditch. She didn't know if the monster was chasing her or not, but she didn't dare risk looking back. Using the little light from the moon that slithered through the trees, she ran.

Exploding through the trees, she collapsed into a clearing, chest heaving. Rolling onto her back, she stared into the darkness behind her. In the distance, the crackle of her burning car was dying down, its orange light wrestling for life against the encroaching darkness.

Pushing herself backward, she staggered to her feet. Her mind raced.

What was that thing?

Did it kill all those people?

Regan's chest heaved up and down. Standing there, ankle deep in the mud, she couldn't help but think about all those gym sessions she had skipped. In the dying light of the car fire, she could see something clinging to the back of her arm.

Slowly, she reached out and grabbed it. The substance came away without any resistance. It's wet, rubbery texture caused Regan to gag. She held it up to the fire light and her blood ran cold.

It was a chunk of human skin.

Regan screamed and threw it away from her. She scrambled backward, wiping away the gore that clung to her clothes and hair. Bile exploded upward. For the second time tonight, she heaved onto the ground at her feet.

"Mommy?" An innocent voice asked.

Regan spun around to see her son standing in the shadows of some nearby trees. The little boy stepped out of the trees and into the moonlight. Regan matched his step forward with a step away from him.

"Mommy, are you ok?" Charlie asked, looking hurt by her retreat.

The images of the demonic creature mimicking her son flashed in Regan's mind. She took another half-step back, preparing to run back into the trees.

The boy took another step forward. "Mommy?" Tears streamed down the kids face. Dirt and mud-coated his face and shirt. "Where are you going?"

Regan took another step back, then stopped.

The little boy had a cast.

Relief flooded Regan's body. She burst into tears, not bothering to wipe them away as she exploded into a sprint toward her boy.

She crashed into Charlie, lifting him off his feet and embracing him in a deep hug. Her tears soaked into his shirt as she wept into his little shoulder.

"Charlie!" She sobbed. "Where were you?"

He peeled his head back to look into his mother's face.

"I was here the whole time." He cried. "You ran away from me!"

Regan looked at the boy, a confused look on her face. "No, I didn't!" She protested.

Charlie raised his tiny hand and pointed at something behind her. "You followed him." The boy whispered.

Regan spun around, nearly tripping in the mud.

Her son, or something that looked like her son, was standing within the treeline, peering out from behind some bushes. Its soulless black eyes stared daggers into Regan and her son.

The Charlie thing leaned forward, falling onto all fours. It's arms broke, the cracks echoing through the woods. The creature writhed in pain as its limbs extended unnaturally.

Regan's breath froze in her chest. Her mind begged for her to run, but her legs didn't respond. She watched in horror as the Charlie thing's face morphed through a series of random facial features before finally settling on an amalgamation of childish features. The creature screamed then returned its gaze to Regan.

"Mommy." Charlie whispered in her ear. "There's a car." He pointed his little finger behind her.

Regan glanced over her shoulder. The warm glow of headlights crested the ridge above them. Subconsciously, she sized up the steep embankment between her and the road. Looking back at the monster, she saw it had followed her gaze.

There was a momentary pause. It was as if the creature was waiting for Regan to make a decision. She made her choice and in a second, the illusion of frozen time vanished.

Regan whirled around and sprinted toward the embankment. Behind her, the creature released a deep wail. It launched itself toward Regan, all four of its limbs pumping. Charlie bounced up and down with each pump of her legs. He screamed and buried his face into the crook of her neck.

Regan reached the embankment and threw herself onto it, Charlie's weight slowing her down. With one hand, she squeezed Charlie to her. With her free hand, she buried her fingers into the mud and rocks, desperately clawing her way toward the road. The rumble of a motor filled the air, the headlights from a truck illuminating the area. Regan breathed heavily, willing herself to move faster.

They had nearly reached the top of the embankment when something wrapped around her leg. It clamped down, sending a wave of pain searing a path through her thigh. She craned her neck to look past Charlie and between her legs.

The creature's long hand had a firm grip on her right ankle, its gnarled fingers digging into her flesh. Her gaze followed the monster's impossibly long arm until she locked eyes with it. The abomination had taken on the face of a little girl. Blonde hair waved around wildly in front of her face. Two bright blue eyes stared back at Regan. The girl smiled, revealing rows of razor sharp teeth that protruded up at all angles.

Without thinking, she dropped Charlie. The boy fell to the dirt with a whimper. She lifted her free leg and launched it backward, connecting with the haunting face of that monstrous little girl. The creature's grip loosened for a brief second.

Regan took the moment to grab her son and push him toward the top of the hill. The truck was close now, the roar of its engine intertwining with the frantic cries of the creature.

"Charlie, run!" She yelled and pointed at the top of the hill to the approaching truck. He followed his mother's instructions without question. On all fours, he scurried up the hill.

The creature jerked its head, morphing from the face of the little girl to a little boy with bright red freckles. It locked its eyes on Charlie and screamed in anger. The monster stretched its limbs, crawling over Regan and racing toward Charlie.

Regan rolled over and grabbed the creature's leg as it passed. She sunk her teeth into the creature's calf and shook her head violently. The monster's thin gray flesh came away from the bone with ease. Black goo gushed from the wound. Regan forced back a gag as the fluid filled her mouth and coated the back of her throat. Fighting the urge to pull away, she bit down harder, tearing into thick, stringy muscle.

The creature threw its head back and howled in agony. It kicked its leg, yanking it from Regan's mouth. With another mighty kick that connected firmly with Regan's chin, she felt herself flying through the air. She smashed against the ground, expelling the air from her lungs. Gasping for breath, she looked up toward her son. He was about to reach the top of the hill, the monster right behind him.

Ignoring the crippling pain in her chin, she jumped to her feet. Regan sprinted up the hill, but immediately realized she wouldn't make it in time. Her eyes darted around for anything she could use to distract the creature. In her hasty scan, she almost missed it. A smooth rock, about the size of a softball, sat on the ground about a foot away. She lunged for it. The rock was a little heavier than a softball. Self-doubt crept into the back of her mind. Regan hadn't thrown a softball in years, but muscle memory kicked in. She spread her legs, reared back and threw the rock as hard as she could.

The rock smashed into the back of the creature's head just as it was reaching out to grab Charlie. An explosion of black goo filled the air. The monster stumbled and slid a few feet back down the hill. Grabbing the open wound on the back of its head, it looked down at Regan, then back up at Charlie. The monster slammed its fist into the ground, crying out in frustration.

Charlie reached the top of the hill and climbed over the guardrail, disappearing from view. The squeal of brakes locking up replaced the monster's shouts.

Regan could hear the faint sounds of a man talking, followed by Charlie's sobs. She couldn't make out exactly what the boy was saying but a moment later, a man appeared at the guardrail. He leaned over it, silhouetted by the headlights from his truck. It took a moment for Regan to make out his features.

It was Doug.

A look of abject terror spread across his face when his eyes fell on the monster between himself and Regan. Its face shifted again, taking on the appearance of a young hispanic boy with short, black hair.

The creature looked back and forth between Regan and Doug several times. It dropped its head and growled, anger evident in its voice. Without looking back at them, it turned and sprinted into the woods. Its shouts filled the air as it disappeared from sight.

With a sigh of relief, Regan clambered to her feet and limped up the embankment. Doug wordlessly helped her over the guardrail and into the front seat of his truck. It smelled of cigarette smoke and burnt oil. Regan held Charlie in her lap as Doug gently turned the truck around.

"What made you come after us?" Regan whispered.

"I had a bad feeling." Doug said flatly. "Too many missing children in this valley." He paused and looked out the window at the wide expanse of wilderness that stretched out below them.

"Now I know why." He muttered to himself.

They flew past the wooden sign that marked the entrance to the Valley of Missing Children as they headed back toward the gas station. Regan noticed something different from this angle.

The back of the wooden sign was covered in missing persons posters.

Nearly all of them were children.

The Grotto

"Throw another one." Tank whispered.

Jerome bent over and picked up the smallest pebble he could find out of the garden. He tossed it up and down a few times in his right hand, judging it's weight. Cocking back, he launched it toward the second-story window. It pinged off the glass with a cracking noise and for a brief second, Jerome was afraid he had broken the window.

The boys waited with anticipation as the humid Florida air seeped into their clothes. This, along with the excitement of sneaking out caused Jerome to break out into a heavy sweat. He could feel cool beads of sweat running down his back as he stared up at the window.

"Is this kid deaf?" Hector asked.

Tank shrugged, bending over to grab another pebble. "The little bitch is probably chickening out." He selected a slightly larger pebble and chucked it at the window. It smacked into the glass with a loud ping. Tank tracked it with his eyes as it fell back to the ground. Moving forward, he stepped on some neatly manicured flowers, trampling them to the ground.

"Watch out for the flowers." Hector hissed.

Tank picked up the pebble, then shot his friend a dirty look. "You're worried about the flowers?" He asked incredulously. "With what we are about to do, you're worried about the flowers?"

Hector dropped his head. "His mom probably cares about those flowers." He mumbled, toeing the dirt with his shoe.

Tank cocked back the pebble, launching it toward the window. The window slid open as the rock left Tank's hand. It sailed through the air, connecting squarely with Samuel's forehead. The boy grunted and fell back into his room.

Tank spun on his heels with his arms outstretched. "I think I just killed Sam."

The other two boys chuckled. "Not yet," Hector whispered.

Samuel appeared in the open window again, still rubbing his forehead. Leaning his head out, he waved at the boys.

"I'll be down in a second." He said with a huge smile.

"Dude, shut up!" Jerome half whisper shouted.

Samuel's face turned red. He flashed the boys a thumbs up and disappeared back into the darkness of his room, not bothering to close his window.

The sound of his bedroom door squealing as Samuel opened it drifted through the open window.

Hector shook his head. "This nerd is going to get us busted."

"Nah." Tank said coolly. "Besides, we need him for the ritual."

Samuel appeared at the sliding glass door on the first floor. The boy paused, typing a code into a panel on the wall, deactivating the security system. He grabbed the door handle and froze. Slowly, he looked back over his shoulder.

Unable to see what Samuel was looking at, Hector nervously shifted his weight from one foot to the other. He glanced at the trees at the back of the property. As the fastest kid in school, he could easily reach the treeline before Samuel's parents got a good look at him. He took a half-step toward the back of the property.

After a tense moment, Samuel gingerly slid the door open. Turning his body sideways, he scooted through the narrow opening and closed the door behind him. Once he was through, he gave the other boys a huge smile and another thumbs-up.

"This kid sucks." Jerome whispered to Tank.

Tank nodded, then stepped forward, holding his fist out to Samuel.

Samuel gave him a fist bump, then turned to Jerome, holding out his fist. After an awkward pause, Jerome relented and fist bumped him. Samuel repeated the process with Hector.

"You got a sacrifice?" Tank asked.

Samuel nodded. He swung his backpack from around his shoulder and unzipped it. Reaching inside, he withdrew a plastic case.

"It's a Babe Ruth rookie card." He whispered. "My dad gave it to me before... you know..." He looked down at the ground before returning the card to his backpack.

Tank did know.

Samuel's dad had died a year prior in a car accident. Tank's dad was a cop and worked the scene. He remembered his dad describing the scene to his mother. The drunk driver. The head-on collision. The bodies.

Tank shook it off and patted Samuel on the shoulder. "Do you know what you're going to wish for?" He asked.

Samuel shrugged. "I'll figure it out as we walk." Looking back up at Tank, his embarrassment faded. "What did you guys bring?"

Tank shook his head. "No time." He snapped. "Let's go." Without waiting for a response, he turned and jogged across the yard toward the trees. He quickly located the path they had carved while sneaking through the woods. Dipping under a branch, he slipped out of view.

Hector and Jerome followed him. Samuel lingered behind, glancing over his shoulder toward his house.

"You coming or not?" Hector scolded.

Samuel took a deep breath and plunged into the darkness of the woods.

The boys walked in a single-file line toward the north. Sweat formed on Samuel's palms. He had never explored these woods, despite living here his entire life. Now, he was marching through the thick of it, tripping over roots and trampling branches, following three boys he barely knew.

They continued their trek in a line, guided only by a small flashlight in Tank's hand and a few beams of moonlight stabbing through the trees.

Pain began radiating through Samuel's feet. Unlike the others, he wasn't an athlete. He preferred video games and comic books to sports. The others didn't seem at all bothered by the arduous journey. Multiple times, he considered asking the boys for a break but knew they would tease him relentlessly. Samuel already felt strange about hanging out with the popular kids and didn't want to give them a reason to stop talking to him. Realizing these guys were the closest thing he had to friends, he hung his head. At that moment, Samuel decided he would wish for these guys to be his best friends forever.

"We're almost there, guys. Not much further." Tank said.

The sound of his voice breaking through the near-total silence of the forest caused Samuel to jump. He felt his heart slamming against his chest. Glancing up, he saw Jerome smiling over his shoulder at him.

"What's the matter, man?" Jerome asked in a condescending voice. "Scared of the dark?"

Samuel's brain fired on all cylinders, searching for a suitable comeback. Stumbling over his words, he settled on the best rebuttal he could think of. "Nah, just your face." He said.

Hector burst out in obscene laughter. His obnoxious cackling filled the air, echoing off the trees.

"The fuck are you laughing so hard at?" Jerome nearly yelled.

Samuel tensed up, sensing the anger in his new friend's voice. Jerome's head jerked back and forth from Hector to Samuel and back again. It was as if he was trying to decide who to hit first.

"He said he was scared of your face." Hector said through a laugh. "Which is funny because it's too dark outside to actually see you!" He shouted and slapped his knee.

Smacking his lips, Jerome shook his head. "Man, shut your racist ass up!" He balled up his fists and jogged toward Hector.

Throwing his hands up in surrender, Hector stepped back. "Sorry, man. I don't want to fight you."

Dropping his fists, Jerome kicked at the ground, sending dead leaves and dirt raining onto Hector's legs.

Starting to laugh again, Hector covered his mouth. "Besides, it wouldn't be a fair fight." He stifled a chuckle.

Jerome pointed a finger at his friend. "Don't you say it." He shook his head violently. "Don't you fucking say it."

Bursting out in laughter, Hector dropped his hands and ran off into the darkness. "I can't fight you in the dark because I can't see you."

"Son of a bitch." Jerome said through clenched teeth. He leaned forward and sprinted toward Hector. He had made it about twenty yards when Tank yelled.

"Hey! Quit messing around." Tank nodded toward some bushes. "We're here."

Jerome quit running and looked at Tank. Tank had stopped walking and was now standing with his arms crossed over his chest. Jerome turned back to Hector and pointed at him.

"I'm getting you back for that shit later."

Still smiling, Hector returned to the group. "Promises." He laughed.

Despite the absurdity of it all, Samuel smiled too. This was the camaraderie he had been missing out on. The closest he got to this playful level of banter and wrestling was with his little sister. Unfortunately, those matches always ended with his sister in tears and Samuel confined to his room for the evening.

When the other three boys caught up to Tank, he uncrossed his arms. "Alright, the Grotto is just past these shrubs." He threw his thumb over his shoulder to emphasize the correct direction. "Does everyone know what to do?"

Hector and Jerome nodded.

When Samuel didn't respond, all three of their gazes landed on him. He shrunk under their scrutiny, subtly shifting his weight away from them.

"Alright." Tank said in an exasperated voice. "Let's break this down real quick." He angled his flashlight up, allowing the beam to illuminate his face. "This is not a joke. You have to do exactly what I say when I say it. Got it?" His eyes bounced across the other boys. When nobody protested, he continued. "My brother explained everything to me. Him and his friends did this when they were our age." Lowering the flashlight, Tank used it to point towards a walkway. He knew from experience that it would lead them to the mausoleum. "When we go in there, we look down at our feet the whole time." Pointing at Samuel, he said, "You'll go first. You walk up to the altar, get down on your knees and offer your sacrifice."

Samuel looked confused. He pulled out the baseball card and held it up. "I just set it there?" He asked.

"Yeah." Tank replied. "You set it on the altar and say your wish." Glancing up at Jerome and Hector, he gave them a knowing smile. "My brother said the bigger the sacrifice, the more likely the witch is to grant your wish."

"Wi-witch?" Samuel stammered. "You didn't say anything about a witch."

Tank rolled his eyes. "Come on, man. We're talking about magic. What did you think?" He shook his head and pinched the bridge of his nose between his fingers. "Alright. I'm going to keep this short because we don't have all night." Tank pushed a tree limb out of the way, allowing the boys to see down into the grotto, where a large stone building peeked up from the surrounding shrubbery. "Like a thousand years ago there was a witch that lived out here. She used to make potions and shit. I don't really know." He waved his hand dismissively. "Anyway, people would bring her gifts and she would give them stuff." He shrugged his shoulders. "I'm not sure of the details, but I do know some men in the town burned her alive and buried her ashes in that," he paused and pointed at the stone structure, "mausoleum."

Jerome smacked Hector on the arm. "This is so cool." He excitedly whispered.

Samuel didn't seem as excited as the others at the prospect of asking an ancient witch for favors. Clenching his baseball card tight to his chest, he looked from the stone grotto stretching out before them back to Tank.

Sensing his fear, Tank stepped forward and placed his arms on the smaller kid's shoulders. He bent at the waist, bringing himself to eye level with Samuel. "Don't worry, man. We will be right behind you."

Nodding, Samuel took a deep breath. He locked eyes with his friends. "Promise?" He asked.

Tank nodded. "Just go down, kneel in front of the altar. Set your card down and say your wish out loud." He allowed his hands to slide off the boy's shoulders. "If she's happy with your offering, she grants your wish."

Samuel swallowed hard. "And if she doesn't?"

Tank raised an eyebrow. "If she doesn't, what?" He asked.

"If she doesn't like my offering." Samuel said.

Jerome punched Samuel on the arm. It was a playful punch, but it sent a shockwave rolling through Samuel's skinny arms. "Then she drags you to Hell, Sammy!" Jerome teased.

Snapping his attention to Jerome, Tank stuck a finger in his face. "Stop messing with him." He commanded.

Jerome smacked his lips together and waved his hand. "Whatever, man. Let's just get this done. I need to get back before my parents wake up."

Tank nodded. "You first." He said, pulling a branch aside for Samuel.

Samuel took a deep breath, steeled himself, then marched into the grotto.

It wasn't at all like he had expected. He imagined the area looking more like a haunted graveyard from one of the old movies his dad used to watch. Instead, it looked more like a gothic art project. Ornate, stone pillars stretched into the darkened sky, signaling the entrance to the grotto. A concrete sidewalk carved a path through various stone benches, hand-chiseled statues, and signs.

He glanced over his shoulder to confirm the other boys had followed him in. He saw Tank's large frame heading toward him. The boy was obscured in darkness, his outline silhouetted against the moonlight. He held something round in his hand.

Samuel assumed it was a baseball, probably Tank's offering to the witch. He remembered hearing about Tank hitting a home run recently. Smiling, Samuel continued walking down the sidewalk. That baseball was probably Tank's most prized possession.

The stone mausoleum rose up from the darkness of the surrounding woods like an apparition. With each step, Samuel took in more of its design.

Stone walled in three sides of the building, leaving the front open. Old, rusted bars covered the front with only a small opening in the center. To Samuel, it looked as if someone had cut the bars. It brought him a strange sense of comfort. If others really had done this before them, maybe it was safe after all. When he was a few feet away, he began to notice the runes carved into the walls. He examined them as he approached. Deep grooves snaked their way through the stone, adorning the walls in intricate patterns Samuel didn't recognize.

He paused in front of the bars, straining his eyes to make out anything inside the cavernous opening. "Do I just go in?" He asked without looking back.

"Yeah, man." Tank's voice rang out from behind him. Samuel could feel Tank's looming presence hanging over him. The boy had closed the distance between them, his breathing growing louder in Samuel's ears.

Samuel ran his fingers along the rusty bars, dragging them down toward the opening someone had cut. The ancient iron felt rough against his soft hands, and when he pulled them away, they were coated with brown residue. Samuel dipped down and carefully stepped through the opening. He felt the jagged edges of the broken bar stabbing into his back. Making himself as small as possible, Samuel wiggled his way into the mausoleum. He took a few more steps to make sure he cleared the metal bars and slowly stood to his full height.

Despite the open bars, the air smelled musty and old. The stone walls seemed to amplify the sounds around him. Water dripped somewhere deep within the recesses of the building, the splashes echoing off the walls.

"Keep going." Tank ordered.

Samuel glanced over his shoulder to see the much larger boy trying to squeeze his way through the tiny opening. His back brushed dangerously against the broken bar, its jagged edges slicing into his shirt. Stepping aside, Samuel waited for Tank to make his way inside. Jerome and Hector appeared outside the iron gates.

"You first, Pendejo." Hector muttered.

Jerome bent over and stepped into the opening. He paused halfway through and looked back at Hector. "I'm going to hit you for that later." He warned, then finished crawling through the bars.

Despite being bigger than Jerome, Hector navigated the bars more elegantly. He easily bent and moved, displaying a high level of flexibility. Once through, Hector patted Tank on the shoulder.

Motioning with his empty hand, Tank whispered to Samuel. "Lead the way, bro."

Samuel looked deeper into the mausoleum, his eyes adjusting to the little light they had. He placed his hand on one of the walls and stepped forward. Using the smooth stone as a brace and guide, Samuel tip-toed deeper into the crypt.

"Be careful." Tank whispered.

No sooner had he said it than Samuel tripped, nearly tumbling down a rocky staircase. Every fiber in Samuel's being told him to turn back. He knew this was too dangerous. Too over the top. But he also knew this might be his only chance to make friends. Taking the stairs one careful step at a time, he continued the journey into the belly of the mausoleum.

The steps seemed to stretch on forever. Any time he thought he was close to the bottom, there was another set of stairs. They marched deeper underground, seemingly heading toward Hell.

When they finally reached the bottom, Samuel sighed in relief. His mind was already ten steps ahead and he was thinking about how hard it would be to go back up those stairs at the end of the night. His legs would be sore for a month.

Samuel turned to ask Tank what to do next when something hard smashed into the side of his head. The world tilted sideways and swirled around him. His balance waned, sending him crashing to the floor. Samuel's face smashed off the concrete. He felt the warm spray of blood from his shattered nose before he felt the pain. Pain that seared a path across his temple and face. He let out a painful moan. His hands didn't seem to want to respond and for a brief moment, he was afraid he'd been paralyzed. The fear washed away when the feeling in his hands came rushing back.

Someone had ahold of his arms and was yanking them behind his back. He tried to pull his arms away, but whoever the person was had a firm grasp on them. He felt something metallic slide over his wrist, followed by the clicking sound of handcuffs locking into place.

"Tank?" He mumbled.

"Holy shit, man!" Hector exclaimed. "You fucking smoked him."

Samuel's conscious mind wrestled for dominance against the haze in his concussed head. *Had Tank hit him? Why would he do that?*

"Shut up and help me pick him up." Tank said.

From somewhere behind him, a flashlight clicked on, bathing the room in garish yellow light. The sudden brightness burned Samuel's eyes, momentarily blinding him.

Jerome appeared at Samuel's side, hooking one of his arms under the injured boy's shoulder. Tank grabbed the other. Together, they lifted Samuel off the ground.

Dizziness swam through Samuel's head as he rose. The room continued swaying and shifting before him. Propelled forward by the two boys, Samuel tried to work his legs, only for them to turn to Jello-O. They gave out under his weight, sending him crashing back to the floor.

Tank maintained his firm grip, holding up most of Samuel's weight while Jerome struggled to catch his share.

"Pick him up." Tank ordered through gritted teeth.

"I'm trying!" Jerome shot back. "The skinny bitch is heavier than he looks."

Shaking his head, Tank grunted. He dragged Samuel toward an altar at the back of the room. When they reached the stone slab, Jerome dipped down and grabbed Samuel's feet. Together, they hoisted him into the air and dropped him onto the slab.

The jarring impact of being thrown onto stone expelled the air from Samuel's lungs. He launched into a coughing fit. Trying to sit up, he realized his hands were pinned painfully against his back. The metal cuffs dug into the skin of his wrists.

"What're you doing?" Samuel managed to mumble.

"We needed a sacrifice." Tank said flatly. "My brother said, 'The bigger the sacrifice, the bigger the reward.' So, we brought the biggest sacrifice we could think of."

The beam of Hector's flashlight danced around the room and for the first time, Samuel became aware of the seemingly random objects spread around. Baseball cards, an autographed football, a girl's bracelet. The objects littered the floor, evidence of decades of sacrifices to the witch.

Tank's words finally clicked in Samuel's mind.

They're going to kill me.

Samuel thrashed, tossing his shoulder to the side, he tried to roll off the altar.

Tank moved quickly. He grabbed Samuel's shoulder, pinning him to the stone. Raising his fist, he brought it down on Samuel's face.

The fist connected with the boy's already broken nose, causing his head to snap back into the altar. Another bolt of pain ripped a path across Samuel's face. Tears pooled up in his eyes, threatening to spill over.

"Light the candles." Tank said.

Jerome produced a light from his pocket. It was an old-looking flip lighter like Samuel had seen in movies. The boy brushed his thumb against the spark wheel. It took him three times before it finally caught.

Samuel's battered mind drifted. It fixated on the dancing flame as Jerome carefully escorted it around the room. He held it up to a candle. Once it lit, he moved on to another.

With each successive candle, the darkness faded. Samuel's concussed mind pieced the scene together. Metal rods supporting candles jutted from the stone, creating a concentric pattern leading to a statue.

The stone statue stood tall behind the altar. Its lifeless stone eyes stared down at the injured Samuel without pity. Angel wings fanned out from its back, contrasting with the devilish horns on its head.

Samuel's eyes drifted down to the statue's hands. They were holding an urn. For some reason, he had expected the urn to be gaudy, but it was the exact opposite. Its smooth yellow porcelain had no markings or decoration.

Tank moved around the altar, causing Samuel to flinch. The large boy approached the statue and knelt down in front of it. Raising a hand, he let it hang in the air for a moment before resting it on the urn.

"My name is Tommy, but everyone calls me Tank." He whispered, lowering his head. "I'm here to offer a sacrifice." Tank paused and glanced over his shoulder at Samuel.

Samuel shook his head violently. "Please." He whispered.

Tank turned back to the urn and lowered his head again. "I ask you to grant me the wish of making it to the NFL." His voice quivered. "I want to be a professional football player." Tank jerked his hand off the urn, turning his palm over to look at it. He scooted away from the statue and stood up. Slowly turning, he extended his hand for the other boys to see.

"It fucking burned me!" Tank shouted. An enormous grin spread across his face. "I told you it's real!"

Jerome reached over and grabbed Tank's wrist. He pulled Tank's hand closer, inspecting it. His eyes shot up to Tank. "Holy shit, Dude!" He released Tank's hand and rushed around the side of the altar.

Dropping to his knees, he lowered his head. He sucked in a deep breath. Raising his trembling hand, he gently placed it in the urn.

"Um, my name is Jerome. I'm bringing you a sacrifice." Jerome glanced over his shoulder at Tank.

Tank motioned with his hands, encouraging his friend to finish.

Closing his eyes again, Jerome continued. "I ask that you grant me a wish. I want to be a famous baseball player." Mimicking his friend, Jerome yanked his hand away from the urn. He hissed in pain, holding it up for his friends to see.

"Yes!" Tank yelled, pumping his fist into the air.

"Last but not least!" Tank said. He grabbed Hector by the shoulders, massaging his traps as he pushed him toward the statue.

Hector allowed his friend to guide him to the spot. Dropping to his knees, he lowered his head. Hector sat there for a while, not doing anything.

"You good, man?" Tank asked.

Hector nodded. "Yeah, man. I can wish for anything?"

Tank nodded, then realizing Hector couldn't see him, said, "Whatever you want."

Hector nodded. He placed his hand on the urn. "Hi. Um, my name is Hector. My dad, he, um, he has cancer."

He paused when he heard Jerome whispering something behind him.

"Dude, shut up." Tank whispered.

Hector waited a moment longer to make sure Jerome wouldn't interrupt him again. "I offer this sacrifice for you to get rid of my dad's cancer."

The urn shook slightly, then glowed a bright red. Hector ripped his hand away, hissing at the pain.

Holding his palm up to his friend, he smiled. "This shit is going to work!"

Samuel had remained silent during the entire ritual. A part of him was still hoping this was some elaborate prank. He thought they would torment the nerdy kid, make him pee his pants, then tell everyone at school about it. He'd done this song and dance a million times before, but this was different. The burned hands and eager wishes finally broke through his psyche, convincing him things were real.

He tried to sit up, managing to get his shoulders a few inches off the altar. Tank snapped in his direction. The enormous boy brought his fist down like a hammer, slamming it into Samuel's chest. Samuel grunted and crashed back to the cold stone.

"You're not going anywhere, Sammy." Tank said flatly.

Samuel gasped for air. Between gasps, Samuel managed to squeak out a protest . "You don't have to do this." He pleaded. Unable to hold it back any longer, tears rolled down his cheek. They started slow at first but grew faster with every passing second.

"It's too late for that, man." Hector said as he patted Samuel's leg.

Seizing the opportunity, Samuel kicked as hard as he could. His heel landed firmly against the boy's chest. Hector stumbled backward, tripping over a rock and crashing to the floor.

Jerome lunged forward and backhanded Samuel across his face. His knuckle connected firmly with Samuel's lip.

Samuel's head snapped to the left. Burning pain ripped through his torn lip. Blood spurted from his mouth, decorating the stone floor in gore.

"Ahh!" Samuel groaned.

Hector stood up, his face burning with fury. His nostrils flared as he approached the altar. "You're fucking dead, kid." Hector snarled.

Samuel squirmed away, trying to work his way off the altar. Tank grabbed a handful of his hair and jerked his head back to the altar. "Not so fast." Tank taunted.

Hector closed the distance between them. Raising up his hands, he swung wildly. His fist connected with Samuel's stomach in a flurry of vicious impacts.

"Please!" Samuel shouted. "Just stop!"

Hector pulled back and punched Samuel between the legs.

Samuel broke into a series of groans, rolling as much onto his side as Tank would allow. Drool dripped from his mouth, mixing in with the blood.

Hector moved to punch Samuel again, but Tank placed a hand on his chest. "That's enough, bro." Tank shook his head. "Let's just do this thing."

Hector lowered his fist. "Fine." He mumbled, moving into position next to Tank.

Jerome looked like he was about to vomit. His eyes floated from the staircase to Samuel and back to the staircase.

Seeing his friend's hesitation, Tank's lip twitched. "It's too late for that, Jerome."

Jerome shifted his gaze to meet Tank's. Tank's eyes were filled with vitriol. Lowering his head, he stepped up to the altar.

"Alright. My brother said there are two rules." Tank leaned forward so he could see both his friends. Ignoring Samuel's groans, he continued. "First, we all have to participate."

Samuel tried to roll off the table again. Tank reached out and grabbed his shoulder.

"Please, just let me go." He cried.

Tank shoved Samuel back to the altar. "You got that Jerome?" He asked.

Jerome didn't look up. He slowly nodded his head, fighting back the urge to vomit.

"Alright, rule number two." Tank said, holding out the fingers. "My brother said once the ritual starts, you have to keep your eyes closed the entire time."

"What happens if we open our eyes? Hector asked.

"I don't know, man. You'll die or something."

"Keep my eyes shut. Got it." Hector said.

"You guys ready?" Tank asked.

"Please!" Samuel shouted. "You don't have to do this!"

Reaching into his pocket, Tank withdrew a kitchen knife. Its slender black handle fit neatly into his hand. The light of the candles reflected off its stainless steel, giving it the impression of being on fire.

Samuel's eyes stretched wide. His heart smashed against his chest, matching with his rapid breathing.

"Remember, once you stab him. Eyes closed." Tank whispered.

Tank raised the knife above Samuel.

"No. No. No." Samuel mumbled. His panicked thoughts prevented him from formulating coherent sentences.

Tank closed his eyes and envisioned himself coming out of a tunnel in a Seattle Seahawks jersey. In his mind, he sprinted onto the field, helmet on, thrusting his fist into the air to the cheers of seventy thousand people.

With a smile on his face, he plunged the knife into Samuel's stomach.

The blade sliced into Samuel's stomach with ease, the entire blade disappearing into the skin above his belly button. There was a moment where nobody moved. Tank held the knife there, unsure what to do next. Blood bubbled up to the surface around the wound and spilled over. Red rivers carved a path across Samuel's pale stomach, racing down to the altar. When the first drop of blood hit the stone slab, it was as if the trance was broken.

Samuel released an anguished cry. It filled the mausoleum, echoing off the cold stone walls and out into the night air. He craned his neck to get a look at the injury, but the tightening of his abs sent a shock wave of pain rippling through his body.

Tank pinched his eyes shut and ripped the knife from Samuel's stomach. A spray of crimson streaked out with the knife. It splattered across the statute's face. Bloody tears dripped down its cheeks.

"Here." Tank said. He held out the knife to Hector. "Take it." He whispered.

Hector almost didn't hear his friend over Samuel's agonized cries. He cracked his eyes but was very careful not to look at the urn. He saw Tank's hand, coated in a thick layer of blood. The knife's shiny blade shimmered red in the candles glow.

Hector felt a bead of sweat run down the center of his spine. The frigid tomb was now awash with sweltering heat. He could feel the temperature rising with every passing second.

He snatched the knife from Tank. Not wanting to give himself an opportunity to back out, he thrust the knife toward Samuel. The blade connected with Samuel's side, just above the hip.

Samuel's screams rose into a crescendo. The boy screamed for help and pleaded for his life.

Hector yanked the knife out again. A tidal wave of blood escaped the gash. It flooded over the side of the altar, coating Hector's shoes. The warm liquid absorbed into the fabric, causing his toes to stick together. Bile rose in the back of Hector's throat. His stomach cramped. Unable to hold it back, he held out the knife to Jerome.

Jerome quickly took it, trying to ignore the splattering of Hector's vomit as it intertwined with Samuel's screams and the steady dripping of blood onto the stone floor.

Jerome looked down at the knife and noticed the room was growing brighter now. He fought the urge to look up, but could feel the heat from the candles as their flames grew larger. Somewhere in the recesses of his mind, he heard a woman's voice.

It was singing. He lingered there, holding the knife in his hand, its heavy blade counter balanced by the handle. The singing in his head grew louder, drowning out the screams. Drowning out Hector's heaves. Drowning out the steady dripping of blood. It rose into a rhythmic dance in his head and that's when he realized it.

It wasn't singing.

It was chanting.

Every inch of Jerome's body willed him to drop the knife and run out of the mausoleum. An image of himself running naked through the forest flashed in his mind. He saw himself from a bird's eye view, watching his naked, blood-soaked body sprinting between the trees. The woman's chants grew louder. It beckoned him. It called out from somewhere beyond, begging him to give in.

And so he did.

Jerome lifted his head and opened his eyes.

To his horror, the statue was smiling. The flames on the numerous candles had grown impossibly high. The tips of the fire licking the roof. Somehow, there was no smoke. The urn burned a furious red, looking as if it would burst at any second. Jerome flinched, confident the blast would send razoresque shards of ceramic flying at them with breakneck speed.

The chanting in his head continued to grow louder. He couldn't understand the words but knew it was encouraging him. The voice morphed from one to two inside his head. The voices multiplied, a symphony of chanting drowning out Samuel's pleas. He was distantly aware of Tank screaming at him to finish it and through the haze, he did.

Jerome shoved the other two boys aside. He rushed toward Samuel's head, holding the knife out in front of him. Without hesitation, he plunged the knife into Samuel's neck.

Samuel's eyes locked on Jerome's as the boy sucked for air that would never come. The two stood there, embroiled in their desperation. One of them willing the other to die, the other doing anything to stay alive.

The flames of the candles grew dimmer as the light faded from Samuel's eyes. The chanting in Jerome's head faded to a gentle whisper, like a breeze through a field. After another minute, the chanting was gone altogetherer and the candles went out, plunging the cavernous tomb into pure darkness.

The three surviving boys stood frozen in the abyss, nobody wanting to be the first one to break the spell of the silence. Tank removed the flashlight from his pocket and clicked it on.

A beam of garish light streaked through the darkness, illuminating a still-shaking Jerome. His hand lingered above the blade, tears rushing down his face.

"Is it over?" Hector asked. He stood up and wiped chunks of vomit from his chin.

"Uh." Tank muttered. He aimed the flashlight's beam toward the urn. It was resting in the statute's hands as if nothing had happened. He moved the beam around the room; with the exception of Samuel's dead body, everything was exactly the same.

"I think so." Tank said.

"Did it work?" Hector asked.

"It had to have, right?" Tank shrugged. "Y'all felt the heat. That was the witch's magic or something."

Hector lowered his voice. "I hope you're right."

Tank squeezed Hector's shoulder. "Have I ever let you down? Come on. Let's get out of here."

Hector and Tank strutted across the room to the stair-case, pausing when they realized Jerome wasn't following them.

"Jerome." Tank said.

Jerome didn't respond. He lowered his hand, wrapping his fingers around the handle.

"Jerome!" Tank shouted.

The abrupt noise broke the trance Jerome was in. He shook his head and spun on his heels. "Fuck. Sorry." He jogged across the room to the other boys. "I must have zoned out or something."

"It's all good, brother." Tank said, patting his friend's back. "Let's go."

Together, the boys made the arduous climb up the stone stairs. When they emerged from the crypt, they could see the faintest rays of sunlight peeking through the trees. Tank looked down at his watch. "Four AM!" He shouted. "We weren't down there for four hours, were we?" He shouted, his voice cracking in the process.

"Oh, fuck. Oh, fuck." Hector said. He rushed toward the bars and slipped through the opening. The tip of one of the bars knicked his right shoulder, tearing his shirt and drawing blood. He sucked in a short breath. Ignoring the pain he took off, jogging through the grotto.

Tank pushed past Jerome and wormed his way through the narrow open. He proceeded to follow his friend toward the trees.

Jerome approached the bars. He bent to crawl through the broken bars but froze. Just outside the mausoleum, sitting on a headstone, was the witch's urn.

Numbness washed over Jerome, his heart skipping several beats. He forced himself to crawl through the opening, eyes fixed on the urn. When it didn't move, he sprinted after his friends.

Tank and Hector had already reached the forest, disappearing into its thick foliage. Jerome struggled to catch up. His heart slammed against his chest. The overwhelming sense of being watched came over him. He jerked his head frantically from side to side, searching for any sign of the witch. Side-stepping to avoid a tree, he kicked a root. His momentum carried him forward. He fell to the ground, unable to catch himself in time.

The cold forest floor felt good against his flush cheeks. He lay there, attempting to gather his energy.

Somewhere nearby, a twig snapped.

Jerome jerked his head up and immediately felt sick.

In front of him, about twenty feet away, was the statue. It held the urn, not cradled in its arms like before, but out in front of it, as if offering it to Jerome. He pushed himself to his hands and knees, crawling backward away from it.

Reaching a large oak tree, he used it as a brace to help him stand up. He turned to run, but before he could, he heard the chanting again.

This time, it wasn't in his head. It swirled all around him. The witch's cries danced off trees, sending birds flying into the brightening sky. The chants encompassed him, swaddling him in a heavy blanket of words he didn't understand.

Jerome's chest tightened, forcing him to gasp for air. He grabbed his throat, panic washing over him.

Collapsing to his knees, he stretched a hand out, searching for help that would never come.

Blackness encroached on his vision. Jerome felt his body growing weaker. He was about to give in when a woman's voice whispered in his ear.

"You should have kept your eyes closed."

Unable to respond, Jerome slumped to the floor, the darkness of death swallowing him.

Hector sprinted ahead of his friends. He pumped his legs faster, fighting to get home before his parents woke up. Behind him, he could hear Tank shouting for him, but he didn't slow down. If his parents found out he had snuck out of the house, he would be grounded forever.

He exploded through some bushes, stumbling onto the sidewalk. Looking around, he gathered his bearings and took off running again.

The sun was burning off the night little by little as he approached his house.

Hector's heart sank when he saw the kitchen light on. Quietly, he sprinted across the lawn. Two green trash cans rested half-full on the side of the house. Careful to make as little noise as possible, he climbed onto one of the trash cans. Stretching onto his tiptoes, his fingers wrapped around the smooth wood of his window sill. With a little hop, he grasped the ledge and pulled himself into his room.

He worked his way through the open window, forward rolling onto the ground. Jumping to his feet, Hector kicked off his soiled clothes and tossed them into a pile at the back of his closet. He crept across the room to his dresser and pulled out a pair of basketball shorts.

Still trying them around his waist, Hector cracked his bedroom door open. The hallway before him was completely dark.

From downstairs, he heard the clank of dishes on the stove. Hector thought he must be hearing things because nobody had cooked breakfast in this house since his dad got sick.

Hector slid out of his room and into the dark hallway. The soft carpet felt terrific against his sore feet. He reached the staircase and carefully descended the steps.

When he rounded the corner, he couldn't believe his eyes.

His father was standing next to the stove, bouncing his foot to the rhythm of the song playing in his headphones. He grabbed the pan and, with a flick of his wrist, flipped an omelet.

An enormous smile crossed Hector's face.

It actually worked. He thought to himself. He lingered there a moment longer, watching his dad dance in the kitchen. Turning away, Hector made his way back to the stairs, climbing them as quickly as possible. All he needed to do was to slip into the bathroom and wash away the blood and grime.

He was still smiling when he reached the top of the staircase. Seeing something move at the end of the dark hallway, his smile faltered.

"Mom?" He whispered.

No answer. Hector shook his head. He had nearly convinced himself that he had imagined the movement when he saw it again. It was a subtle change in darkness at the end of the hall. It would have been imperceptible if he had not been staring right at it.

His blood ran cold. Slowly, he reached for the light switch. Swallowing hard, he flipped it.

The lights on the roof of the hallway blinked to life, washing the area In fluorescent light. Hector shielded his eyes from the brightness.

Blinking away the stars in his eyes, he returned his gaze to the end of the hallway.

A scream lodged itself in his throat.

At the end of the hallway was what looked like an old woman in a tattered gray dress. Her skin was charred and the stench of burnt meat permeated the hallway.

Acting on instinct, Hector took a half step back, coming dangerously close to the staircase.

The witch's face snapped up to meet his stare. From within her tattered dress, she withdrew something, cradling it in her arms like a baby.

It was the urn, and it was burning bright red.

"I'm coming for all of you." She whispered.

A cacophonous roar erupted in Hector's head, forcing him to grab his temples in pain. The sound of the woman's voice chanting nonsensical words built up in his head. He squeezed his eyes together, begging for any relief from the mounting pressure. When he opened his eyes, he found himself staring into the dark blue eyes of the witch. The stench of her burnt skin filled his nose.

She gave him one last smile and pushed him down the stairs.

Hector tumbled head-first down the stairs. His head smacked against the ground with a sickening crunch and his neck protruded at an impossible angle.

The witch stood at the top of the stairs, her stoic gaze taking in the scene of Hector's ruined body. She bounded down the stairs and fell to the ground next to Hector.

His body twitched uncontrollably as the sensation in his arms and legs faded. The witch leaned in close. Her rancid breath made Hector's eyes water even more than they already were. Sticking out her tongue, she licked Hector's cheek.

"Your friend, Tank, is next." She whispered in his ear. She pulled back, wrapping her thin fingers around his throat and squeezed.

Just before Hector succumbed, the witch smiled.

"This whole town will pay for what it did to me." She hissed.

The Children's Garden

"I'm not sure I can go through with this." Tabby muttered from the back seat of the minivan. She gazed out the window at an old, closed down shopping center. The sign above the building proudly proclaimed it the "Green Cove Shopping Centre." Her mind drifted to what the shopping center used to look like. She remembered coming here with her mother. They would do their grocery shopping at the Green Cove Grocery before going to the video store next door and renting a movie. It was their Friday night routine. One that ended very abruptly.

"Did you hear what I said?" Joshua asked.

Tabby shook her head, her long purple hair whipping from side to side. "I'm sorry, I zoned out for a second."

Miles turned the wheel, accelerating through the one major intersection in town. Tabby wondered how long it took for the town to die after she moved away. The intersection light hung uselessly from a pole, the lights no longer working.

"I said we need you to come through. We sunk a lot of money into this and we are counting on you." Joshua was looking back over his seat now. His tan skin appeared pale in the dying light of the sun. He brushed his curly black hair out of his face. "Seriously, are you good?"

Tabby nodded slowly, returning her gaze to the window. She watched rows of trees zip past. Someone squeezed her shoulder.

"It's going to be ok, Tabby." Erika's soft voice reassured her. Tabby reached up and squeezed the girl's hand. "I'm scared too." She whispered. Holding out her water bottle toward Tabby, she shook it slightly. "Go on, it'll help."

Faking a smile, Tabby took the bottle and unscrewed the lid. She took an enormous gulp, holding it in her mouth for a moment before swallowing. The cool water helped relax her and stifled the rising sense of panic threatening to overtake her. Tabby took one more large swig before screwing the cap back on and passing it to Erika.

"Thank you." Tabby whispered.

Giving her a warm smile, Erika nodded. "No problem."

Miles flipped on the van's blinker. Tabby listened to the incessant clicking as the vehicle veered to the right. She knew they had reached their destination but couldn't bring herself to look at it. Not yet.

The van jolted as it went over a pothole. Recording equipment bounced around in the back, sliding into the side of the van.

"Jesus Christ, Dude!" Joshua shouted.

Miles held up a hand. "My bad."

"Damn right that's your bad. There's expensive shit back there." Joshua shook his head. "Just be careful."

It was Miles' turn to shake his head. "Like I did it on purpose." He muttered.

Ignoring him, Joshua pointed to an area through the windshield. "Let's park over there. It'll be close enough to get the equipment, but the van won't be in any of the shots." The van eased to a stop.

Tabby continued staring out the window. She gazed into the trees in the distance. Nausea broiled in her stomach, threatening to erupt. She couldn't believe she had agreed to do this. Coming back to this place was a huge mistake. It had been ten years to the day since her life was ruined. Since so many lives were ruined.

The van's sliding door opened behind her. She could feel Erika sliding across the bench seat and exiting the car.

"You coming?" Erika gently asked.

Tabby inhaled deeply and nodded. She stared at her feet while she slid across the seat and out into the parking lot.

The black asphalt was cracked and unkempt. Erika took her hand.

"It's ok." Erika whispered. "It's just a building."

Those words danced in Tabby's mind. The sentence seemed unfinished. Erika should have said, *it's just a building that ruined your life*, or maybe, *it's just a building that twenty-five kids died in*. It was spoken like it was no big deal.

Miles and Joshua went to work setting up their cameras and lighting equipment, completely oblivious to Tabby's discomfort. She knew the building and events were meaningful to them. It was clear that the events of that day had a profound impact on all their lives, but none of the others were there that day.

Erika took Tabby's arm and guided her across the parking lot. Tabby kept her eyes trained on her feet, focusing on putting one shoe in front of the other. The nausea she had experienced in the car returned with vengeance. It burned at the back of her throat, causing her mouth to water. Her heartbeat quickened with each step. Despite the cool fall air, sweat beaded up on her back, carving moist trails down her spine.

"Alright, we're almost ready." Joshua said to the group. "Tabby, is this your first time seeing The Children's Garden since that day?" He asked, a hint of disdain in his voice.

"Yes." Tabby mumbled.

"We don't have you mic'd up yet, can you speak up for the camera?"

Tabby's head snapped up. She was greeted by the glaring lens of a camera. It's massive eye peered into her. Her eyes lingered on the camera for a moment before drifting up to the building in the background. She took it all in. The enormous sign that proclaimed it, "The Children's Garden," with the tagline, "where children grow," underneath. Shingles stood missing from a dilapidated roof that threatened to fold in on itself. Plywood boards covered shattered windows. Graffiti, proclaiming the building to be haunted, adorned those boards.

It hit Tabby all at once. Her vision swirled and darkened at the edges. Her knees trembled and buckled, plummeting her to the hard asphalt below. The nausea erupted like a volcano. She spewed outward, subconsciously trying to avoid getting any on her clothes.

Miles and Joshua high-fived above her. "Shit, dude. She actually puked! Did you get that on camera?" Joshua's callous voice asked.

"I sure fucking did, man!" Miles exclaimed.

Erika moved forward, positioning herself between Tabby and the camera. "You guys are fucking assholes!" She shouted. "Shut that shit off for a minute so we can help her."

Miles held up his hands in mock surrender and then tapped a button on the top of the camera. The little red light indicating it was recording went dead. "Sorry, I just thought it would be important to get her reaction to seeing it for the first time."

"Well, you got it." Tabby snapped. She dragged her arm across her face, wiping away chunks of vomit. "I hope it helps to sell your movie." She said it with as much sarcasm as she could muster.

"It's a documentary, not a movie." Joshua said.

Tabby pushed herself off the ground. Erika leaned over and put an arm around her. She helped Tabby stand upright.

"I'm good. I'm good." Tabby insisted, taking a step away from Erika. "Let's just get this shit over with."

Joshua clapped his hands together. "Let's do it!" He turned away from the group and started walking toward the abandoned daycare. "So, here's the deal. Miles and I," he pointed to Miles, then back to himself. "We broke in here last night. We got a ton of B Roll to pad our run time and to use during voiceovers." He reached the front door and gripped the slab of plywood covering it. Giving it a hard tug, he yanked it aside. The glass front door was shattered, giving Joshua an easy way into the condemned building. Joshua held out his hand to display the opening. "All we have to do is shoot both of your parts." He waved his hand in a "come on" motion, then dipped through the broken glass and disappeared into the darkness of the building.

Tabby glanced at Erika, her own hesitation reflected in the woman's eyes. The two lingered there, neither of them wishing to be the first to enter the building.

Behind them, a white light flicked on, casting their shadows against the wall. Tabby looked back, shielding her eyes against the light. Miles held up his camera on a large gimbal, the lens staying steady despite his slight movements.

Erika stuck up her middle finger and jammed it against the camera lens. The camera rocked back, sending the electric gimbal into panic mode. Little engines whirled as it tried to rebalance itself.

"Come on, man." Miles groaned. He held up the camera and double-tapped a button on the back to center it. "You fucked up my shot!"

"Keep pointing that thing in my face and I'll fuck up more than that." Erika growled.

Tabby lowered the hand she had used to shield herself against the blinding light above the camera. Her mind raced. It wasn't too late to walk away. She could climb in the van and wait till they were done shooting. If she waited it out, there would be no significant repercussions. Except the money. The overdue rent bill flicked in her mind. Inhaling deeply, she forced her feet to move. Numbness tingled through her legs as she climbed through the door into the suffocated darkness of "The Garden".

The air in the old daycare was stifling. The malodor of molding and decaying wood hung in the air. Cold air whistled through cracks in the walls, broken windows, and holes in the roof.

Behind her, Miles and Erika were still bickering and Tabby couldn't help but wonder if there was more going on between the two of them than they had let on. Tabby waited patiently as Erika gently crawled through the opening, followed by Miles, his camera leading him.

The light from Miles' camera filled the room, revealing the entrance of the daycare. A large reception desk filled most of the room. Dust coated every surface. Tabby was about to turn and enter the main part of the daycare when something caught her eye. A lone clipboard sat on the desk.

Without intending to, Tabby reached out and touched it. She ran two fingers across the thick layer of grime, wiping it away.

It was a sign-in sheet.

She wiped away more of the grime until she could read the date at the top.

July 25th

Tabby's heart exploded into a furious rage. Sweat welled up under her arms in stark defiance against the cold.

It was *the* sign-in sheet.

Her eyes flicked back and forth across the sheet. The names screamed in her mind as she read them. She scanned the sheet, recognizing some of the names from memory and others from years of trial records. A vein throbbed in her temple, the nausea building up in her stomach again.

Beside her, Erika stepped up to the desk. An audible gasp escaped her lips at the sight of the sign-in sheet. Erika's hand reached out toward the sheet but came up short. It hovered inches above the paper. Her fingers absentmindedly traced one of the names in the air.

Emily Morris.

"Was that your..." Tabby's question drifted off but was answered all the same. Erika couldn't hold on to her "tough girl" exterior. Tears rushed down her cheeks. They clung to her chin before plummeting onto the dust-coated counter.

The two women stood there, lost in their own memories and pain. Their shared misery filled the space between them. Tabby would have been content standing there all night, had it not been for Miles and his camera. He moved around to her left, the camera's light illuminating the desk.

"You're such a dick, Miles." Erika snapped, wiping the tears from her face.

"I'm literally just doing my job." He snapped.

Erika opened her mouth to argue but was cut off.

A bloodcurdling scream erupted from deep within the daycare. Joshua's voice filled the air before drifting off.

Tabby's head snapped toward the screaming. The interior of the daycare was pitch black. There was no sign of Joshua.

"Joshua?" Miles called from behind his camera. He waited for a response that never came, then tried again. "Joshua, you alright buddy?"

Tabby glanced at Erika, her own fear reflected in the woman's eyes. In unison, the two girls whirled back around. The three of them stood there, staring into the darkened doorway.

Something materialized in the darkness. A looming shape darker than the area around it approached. Tabby's breath caught in her throat. Miles scrambled to point his camera light in that direction, nearly dropping it in the process. He regained control and pointed at the approaching figure.

Joshua shielded his eyes from the blinding light. He stared back at the trio with a dumbfounded look on his face.

"Spiders." He said in a nonchalant manner. "I fucking hate spiders."

"You're such a fucking asshole." Erika gasped. "You scared the shit out of us!"

Joshua laughed. He waved them over. "Come on, let's get this over with."

Shaking her head, Erika pushed past Tabby and followed Joshua into the darkness of the daycare. Miles quickly followed suit, forming a single file line. Tabby allowed herself one last glance at the sign-in sheet, the names fading into the darkness as Miles ventured further into the building with his camera. When the light was nearly completely gone, Tabby tore her gaze from the paper and chased after the others.

The layout of the daycare came back to her in a wave of nostalgia. A long hallway stretched from the office to the open area at the back of the building, doors lined the hallway. Some were cracked open to reveal the classrooms; still in the exact same state they were in on that fateful day. It was like peering into a time machine. The chalkboards, the desks, the toys. Memories she didn't know she had, danced in Tabby's mind. She remembered playing with friends, working on her homework, and helping the teachers clean up at the end of the day.

She followed the others past the classrooms and down the hall. They reached the large open area in the back. Tables stretched across the room, plates and cups still strewn about.

Another bout of nausea rumbled in Tabby's stomach as she realized they had left the building exactly as it was. Drifting away from the others, she examined the mess before them. The food had rotted to the point that it was unrecognizable, but Tabby knew what it was. She hadn't eaten chicken nuggets or mac'n'cheese in a decade and probably never would again. Her hand flew to her mouth when she saw the little stuffed fish she used to carry around, lying on the floor. Crouching down, she slowly stretched her hand out toward it, her fingertips brushing against the dust-covered fabric. An involuntary gasp escaped her lips.

Joshua clapped loudly. "Alright. Here's the game plan." He walked over to the double back doors. Moonlight came through the glass panes and illuminated a section of flooring in front of them. "I'm going to stand here, Miles," he paused, looking around. Pointing to an area off to the side, he said, "I want you to set up over there."

Without a response, Miles rushed to the spot Joshua had pointed to and dropped his tripod. He turned off his gimbal and set it aside before screwing his camera into place atop the tripod. Once he was done, he flashed Joshua a thumbs-up.

"Ok, I want you two over there for now." Joshua pointed to a different corner of the room. "When I give you the signal, I want you both to walk around here as I introduce you." He drew an imaginary line with his finger, instructing them to file around the tables. "Got it?" He asked.

Tabby nodded. Erika rolled her eyes. "Let's just get this over with." Taking Tabby's hand, the two girls walked through the maze of tables, careful not to step on any of the clumps of rotting food or dinnerware.

Joshua waited for everyone to get into their places before giving Miles the signal. Miles pressed a button on the side of his camera and a red light blinked to life. Holding his hand up in a "stop" motion, he quickly adjusted a few settings. Once he was confident he had the settings dialed in, Miles dropped his hand and Joshua started talking.

"We've already touched on the horrific events that took place ten years ago at this daycare." He waved one hand, signaling toward the messy clumps of food scattered about. "But just to recap, The Children's Garden was a daycare in Green Cove, Florida." He turned toward the doors that lead into the garden out back. Joshua reached out, lightly running his fingertips against the layer of dust on a glass pane. "The police conducted a thorough investigation and discovered a few things." He turned back to face the camera. Holding up one finger, he continued. "First, the daycare's owner, Rhonda Snyder, was buried under a mountain of debt." Holding up a second finger, he looked back at the two girls in the corner. "Second, the bank was preparing to foreclose on the daycare." He dropped his hand. "Third. That Rhonda poisoned all the kids at the daycare and buried them out back before turning herself in to the police. And finally, that only two people survived this brutal mass murder." Joshua quickly spun and pointed a finger in the girls' direction. "For the first time ever, Tabitha Snyder and Erika Morris are speaking out about the tragic events that unfolded under this roof." Joshua held his hands out, palms up, for dramatic effect.

Miles pressed a button on the camera and the red light went dead. "That was perfect, man! I don't think we even need a second take!" Miles moved from behind the camera and high-fived his friend. "This is going to be solid gold." He muttered to himself as he returned to his spot behind the camera. Picking up the tripod, he moved it a few feet to the left. "I'm thinking we'll have Tabby walk down this row. I can get both the tables in the shot and you'll see all that nasty ass food."

Joshua nodded. "That works for me. Tabby, you just need to walk down this aisle and stop right about here." He stepped forward and used his toe to draw a line in the layer of dust on the ground. "Then I'll just ask you questions."

Tabby took her position at the end of the aisle. Her heart thundered against her chest. The combination of stage fright and being in this forsaken place punished her senses. That feeling of nausea never faded and now it was exacerbated by a shortness of breath. Sweat beads collected at the top of her forehead before plummeting down her face.

"You ok, Tabby?" Miles asked.

Tabby nodded. "Just fine." She muttered. "Can we please just get this done?"

Miles repeated his hand signal before pressing a button on the side of his camera. The blinding light atop the camera exploded to life, followed by the red light blinking on. Miles held his hand in the air momentarily, then dropped it and pointed at Tabby.

The sweat poured freely now, carving moist paths down her face. Sucking in a deep breath, she took one shaky step forward. A bolt of red-hot pain stabbed through her stomach. Her hands instinctively flew to her abdomen, gripping her sides. A painful groan slipped through her lips, but she pressed on, taking another step. The sensation of walking on hot coals tore through Tabby's legs. The burning radiated from her toes, searing a path through her nerves. Her eyes went wide, the feeling of being set on fire overtook her entire body.

"Tabby, are you..." Miles said before Tabby's scream cut him off.

Tabby fell to her knees, her stomach rolling inside her. She grabbed her stomach and screamed. She felt her bowels release as hot shit filled her pants. She felt it running down the back of her legs. Her chest tightened, forcing the air from her lungs. She gasped out for air but found none.

"Holy fuck!" Joshua shouted. "Call an ambulance!"

Miles rushed around the camera, falling to the ground at Tabby's side. Grabbing her shoulders, he tried to lift her up. "I don't have my phone!" He shouted.

"Shit, me either!" Joshua shouted.

Tabby collapsed to the ground, rolling into the fetal position. The veins on her neck protruded as she fought to suck in air. She writhed in pain. Her panic-stricken eyes locked onto Erika. She was standing in the same spot she had been at the back of the room, smiling evilly.

Tabby's muscles seized harder, causing her fingers to curl painfully when she reached out to Miles. A blood vessel ruptured in her right eye. Miles watched as the white was washed away by dark red blood.

"I don't know what to do!" Miles screamed. He pulled Tabby's head into his lap. "Just keep breathing, Tabby! We will get you some help." Tearing his eyes away from the ghastly scene playing out before him, he looked at Joshua. "Go get your fucking phone!" He shouted.

Miles' words jerked Joshua from his shock. He shook his head vigorously, trying to pull himself back to the present. His legs felt numb and heavy, but he forced himself to walk toward the front of the daycare. After a couple of steps, his senses flooded back to him with a furious vengeance. Glancing over his shoulder one last time, he turned and sprinted for the exit. His footsteps rang out along the hallway as he passed empty classroom after empty classroom.

The door to one of the classrooms stood ajar on his right side. He ran past it without a second thought, but as soon as he did, an overwhelming sense of being watched came over him. He pushed the feeling aside and continued to the front office. Exploding through the door, he felt around blindly in the dark, searching for the exit. Joshua cursed himself for not bringing his phone or at least a flashlight. Then he cursed Miles for putting that piece of plywood back over the door. Joshua couldn't understand why Miles would have done that. It made no sense; the town was empty, it wasn't like someone would catch them in the act of breaking in. His fingertips brushed against the dirty desktop. Using it as a guide, he followed it to the wall and then to the door. His hand found the rough material of the plywood and pushed.

It didn't move.

Joshua paused, then pushed again. Still nothing. He took a moment to feel around, making sure he had the right spot. Once he was sure, he pushed harder. His muscles bulged and he released a loud grunt as he thrust himself against the plywood. It didn't even bend. Joshua reeled in confusion. More screams emanated from deeper within the daycare. Miles was calling for him, begging him to get help. Pulling away from the door, he lifted his leg and kicked as hard as he could. A bolt of pain exploded up his leg, but the plywood didn't move. He grimaced and rubbed his right knee. He scanned the area for anything to use, willing his eyes to adjust to the darkness.

Giving up on this plan, he turned to go back into the daycare. He took a single step before a sound stopped him in his tracks.

A giggle drifted through the air.

It was the giggle of a young girl playing tag or jump rope. Joshua's blood ran cold. Freezing in place, he listened for the sound again. The silence of the office was only broken by Miles' loud crying. When no more giggles came, he propelled himself forward, walking quickly down the hallway.

As he passed the rows of classroom doors, another giggle erupted. Joshua whirled his head to his right in time to see the silhouette of a child disappear into one of the classrooms.

"Hey! Who's there?" Joshua shouted. He stood there shrouded in darkness, searching for any sign of the little girl. After a moment, he shook his head and turned to continue his trek down the hall.

A loud creak filled the air, sending a shiver down Joshua's spine. The door to his right had opened a few inches and now hung partially ajar.

"Hel-hello?" He whispered, his voice cracking with fear. "Who's there?" He took a tentative step forward and reached for the door.

"Joshua! Where the fuck are you!" Miles shouted. His cries reverberated off the walls. Joshua snapped his head in the direction of his friend's shouts.

He opened his mouth to yell back when the door in front of him flew open, slamming hard against the wall behind it.

A little girl in a long yellow dress with her hair done up in pigtails stood in the doorway. An inhumanly large smile stretched across her face. The skin on her left hand was a mess of tattered, putrid flesh.

Joshua's mouth still hung open, but he couldn't seem to gather enough oxygen to scream. His hand lingered in the air between them from where he had tried to open the door.

The girl's decaying maw opened to reveal the tattered remnants of a tongue, wiggling wildly between the clumps of bugs that clung to her teeth. Before Joshua could re-act to the ghastly apparition, its ruined hand shot out and grabbed his wrist. With a single pull, the monstrosity yanked him off his feet, dragging him into the classroom.

He found his breath and screamed. "Erika! Miles! Help me!"

Using just her free hand, the little girl rolled Joshua onto his back. She pulled him to the center of the classroom where the rotting corpses of many more children waited. His eyes stretched open wide.

"No, no, no. Please!" He begged.

The children closed in around him, blocking out the ceiling with their morbid visages. He cried out one last time as the children descended upon him.

Miles tore himself away from Tabby's dead body and sprinted down the hallway toward Joshua's screams. They were coming from a classroom on his left. He tried to stop, but slipped in the dirt and grime in front of the door. The full weight of his body came down on his elbow. Blinding pain rolled over him, only to be washed away by the sight before him.

A bright ray of moonlight illuminated a room full of children standing around his friend. Joshua's lifeless body lay limply on the floor. Each child was taking their turn tearing at the flesh. A river of blood spewed forth, carving a path across the dirty floor. He recoiled as it approached, only for a little girl in a yellow dress to step into the puddle. She winked at Miles and slammed the door.

The aching in Miles' arm returned with fury and radiated up into his shoulder. He allowed himself a long, slow blink. His brain couldn't catch up with what he had witnessed. It replayed in his mind like a damaged record player repeating itself in short bursts. With his senses slowly returning, Miles rolled over, propping himself up on all fours. A deep purple bruise on his elbow was already visible. The joint was swelling like a balloon. He grimaced as he forced himself to his feet. His eyes drifted from the now closed door, to the hallway, then back to the door. The image of the little girl closing the door flashed in his mind. Unable to determine if what he saw was real, he grabbed the door handle with his uninjured arm and twisted.

The door flung open, its hinges screaming their protests. His hands flew to his face in an effort to shield himself from the children. When no blows came, he slowly lowered his hands. There were no zombified children or ghosts. The little girl in the yellow dress had vanished, but Joshua's mangled corpse hadn't. Miles stared at the image. It seared itself into his memory. Turning away from the desecrated remains, he vomited onto the floor. Chunks of his dinner intermingled with Joshua's blood, creating a sickly soup at his feet.

Miles stumbled backward through the open doorway, pulling the door shut behind him. He continued backpedaling until his back smashed into the wall behind him. His eyes stayed stretched open wide.

To his right, he heard the shuffle of little feet scurrying around. The sound snapped him out of the stupor he had fallen into. Miles retreated from the sound, moving back toward where he had left Tabby's body. He had nearly rounded the corner of the hallway when the little girl in the yellow dress stepped out of one of the classrooms.

She stood in the center of the hallway, blocking his path. With her little hands folded politely behind her back, she bounced up and down on her tiptoes.

"Would you like to play with us, mister?" She asked. Her innocent sounding voice resonated all around Miles, suffocating him in a blanket of panic.

"No... no, thank you." He stammered. Daring to take another step toward her, he said, "I was just going to get my friend." Miles pointed to the dining area behind her. "Then we can get going."

The little girl's eyes watered up. "You don't want to play with us?" She asked while lowering her head. Her voice quivered as if she were about to cry.

"I just want to leave." Miles said firmly.

The little girl's head snapped back up. Her eyes burned dark red.

Miles stared into those eyes, and for the briefest flash of a moment, he saw Hell and what awaited him on the other side. The red in her eyes faded to their normal blue hue, and Miles saw something else reflected in them.

The army of dead children behind him.

Miles didn't bother looking back at them. He dropped his center of gravity and sprinted at the little girl. She stepped aside, allowing him to pass uncontested.

"Erika!" He screamed. "Help me!"

He reached the end of the hallway and saw Erika standing over Tabby's body, tears streaking down her face. Her face snapped in his direction, terror in her eyes.

Something caught his right foot and pulled. Miles plummeted to the ground. His head smashed off the floor, causing a spider web-like crack to spread across the tile. A burning sensation spread across his forehead as a gash opened up, spewing blood and coating the ground in front of him.

He felt another tug at his ankle, followed by a searing pain in his calf. Looking back, he saw the army of children emerging from the darkness of the hallway and the little girl in the yellow dress biting into his calf. She yanked her head away, tearing flesh from his leg. He watched her chew, the stringy sinew of his muscle dangled from her mouth, coating her yellow dress in blood.

"Erika! Please!" He screamed.

Erika rushed around one of the tables and ran toward him, arms outstretched.

The children reached him before she could. They grabbed his legs and yanked him back into the darkness of the hallway. His fingernails dug into the tiles, tearing away from his hands as he desperately searched for anything to grab onto.

Erika gasped and covered her mouth as she watched the scene play out before her. The children pulled him into the darkness with incredible speed. His screams rang out, echoing down the hallway until he was swallowed by the darkness. She heard a wet, crunching noise emanating from the abyss, and then everything went silent.

Her eyes danced around wildly. Every creak of the old building was amplified in her mind. She backpedaled away from the hallway and back into the cafeteria. Shadows dashed past her. They moved with furious speed, dancing maniacally at the corners of her vision. She continued backpedaling until the back of her heel struck something hard. The jarring impact forced her backward. She lost her balance. A scream escaped her as she fell.

Her ass smacked off the tile with a thud. The hit rippled through her body. A bolt of pain shot up her spine. The shadows seemed to close in all around her, suffocating her. Gathering her senses, she forced herself into a seated position.

Tabby's dead body lay at her feet. The corpse's skin was already gray, the blood pooling to one side of her face. Veins protruded from her neck and her hand remained outstretched.

"I'm so sorry." Erika whispered. Tears streamed from her face. "I shouldn't have done that." Ripping her eyes away from Tabby, she rolled onto her side and forced herself to stand up. She scanned the room for a way out.

The only exit she saw was the double doors that led out the back.

Into the garden.

Titles of various news articles flashed in her mind.

"Woman kills kids, buries them."

"Massacre at the Garden."

Erika's hand drifted to her pocket. She reached in and felt the folded photo in her pocket. Slipping it out, she unfolded it.

The photo was a cut out from one of those news articles that depicted a tent stretched across the garden behind the daycare. Police officers and forensic technicians scurried about, exhuming bodies from the shallow graves that ironically ran parallel to rows of flowers.

Inhaling deeply, she dropped the picture and watched it flutter to the ground. Erika kicked an empty plate out of her way and marched to the back door. The snap of the deadbolt being pulled back rang out through the daycare. She turned the handle and pushed.

The double doors flew open, allowing the cold night air to rush in. The backyard of the daycare was laid out before her. It looked almost identical to her photo. Rows of child-sized holes pockmarked the lawn. Wilted vegetation lined the holes, intermixing with the dead flowers.

Her eyes drifted from the holes to the fence surrounding the property. The faintest hint of a memory came back to her and she knew there was a gate to the left of the daycare. She turned to walk in that direction when a glimpse of movement caught her eye.

The girl in the yellow dress stood in the middle of the graves. She twirled slightly from side to side, allowing her dress to spread around her.

Erika's mouth fell open. Her tears flowed harder. She took a hesitant step toward the girl, followed by a larger one.

"Emily?" She managed to croak out.

The little girl lit up. Her smile stretched wide and she waved.

"Hey, Sissy!"

Erika took another step. "Is that really you?" She whispered, not sure if she had said it loud enough for her little sister to hear.

"Of course it's me, silly." The little apparition giggled.

At the sound of her sister's laughter, all of Erika's inhibitions washed away. She ran to her sister, jumping over one of the graves to get to her. The girl didn't move toward

Erika. She continued twirling her dress until Erika threw herself to the ground at the little girl's feet.

Erika took Emily into a hug and sobbed. "I'm so sorry I stayed home sick that day!" She wailed into the yellow fabric of her sister's dress. "I should have been here with you." Her tears overtook her vision, blinding her to the approaching children.

"It's ok, Sissy." Emily said. Her cold hands rubbed Erika's back. "You're here now. You came back."

Erika tore herself away and wiped her eyes. She sniffled before giving her sister a warm smile. "Yeah, but I gotta go now." She took her little sister by the shoulders, closed her eyes, and rested her forehead on Emily's.

"You're never leaving The Children's Garden." Emily said.

The flat, malicious tone of the girl's voice sent a shiver down her spine. Erika's eyes shot open. Emily's eyes burned a fierce shade of red.

"This is the place where children grow." Emily spat in a voice that wasn't hers. The girl's sweet timbre had been replaced with a deep baritone.

Erika felt hands closing in all around her. They squeezed her arms, shoulders, ankles and legs. Arms wrapped around her torso and tightened around her like a snake. All at once, they pulled.

She was yanked backward, away from her sister. The squeeze of the hands and arms released her, creating the sensation of falling. The sensation was quickly replaced by the realization that she was actually falling.

Walls of dirt rose up in the corners of her vision. She smacked into the hard, cold dirt with her full body weight. Her head cracked against a rock, blurring her vision. Nearly blinded by the impact and concussion, she immediately felt around. Her hands quickly smacked into dirt walls on either side of her. Looking up, she could see the night sky through a rectangular hole. Stars shimmered around the bright glow of the moon.

She sat up, rubbing her head, when a clump of dirt fell onto her. She looked at the dirt in her hands, then up at the opening above her. The faces of dead children stared back at her, their red eyes burning brightly in the night.

They giggled as they pushed dirt into the hole with their bare hands. Clumps of dirt and grass fell all around Erika. Her heart smashed against her chest. She tried to stand up, but couldn't seem to move her legs. The dirt fell faster and heavier, covering her legs completely. With each passing second, the level of the dirt grew higher, rising to her stomach.

Through her concussion induced haze, the realization hit her.

They were burying her alive. She opened her mouth to scream, only to be rewarded with a clump of dirt to the face. The foul soil coated her mouth. She tried to spit it out, but it was useless. The children were frantic now. Their little hands lobbed more and more dirt into the hole. More and more dirt piled in at increasing speeds, matching the children's panicked movements. It encompassed Erika up to the neck, entombing her in an unmarked grave.

She managed one final scream before the dirt covered her completely.

The Town

Amanda leaned back in her seat and let the cold AC wash over her. She glanced down at the screen in the middle of the Tesla's dashboard. It was ninety-five degrees outside. Coming from Ohio, this Alabama heat was unbearable.

"You good, babe?" Chris asked.

Amanda tilted her head to look at her husband. She gave him a sly smile and reached across the car. Placing her hand firmly on the inside of his thigh, she playfully squeezed.

"Just can't wait to get to the fucking beach." She whined. Biting her lip, she winked at him.

Chris glanced down at her hand and traced her arm with his eyes. There was a tingling sensation in his stomach, and he felt himself becoming excited. "What's the first thing you want to do when we get there?" He asked with a hint of excitement.

She giggled. "You."

"Fucking gross!" Tyler shouted from the back seat. He quickly unclipped his seatbelt, letting it smack against the window with a loud clang.

"Watch it, man!" Chris shouted.

Tyler scooted forward in his seat until he could lean between the couple. "You do know that there are other people in the car, right?"

Amanda squeezed Chris' leg tighter, slowly working her hand up his thigh. Chris' face turned bright red and he shifted uncomfortably in his seat. Amanda shrugged and pulled her hand away. "Oh well." She said.

Tyler patted Chris on the shoulder. "Sorry for cock blocking, buddy."

Chris threw on the blinker of the Tesla and eased the car onto an exit. Shaking his head, he looked into the rearview. "No, you're not." He scoffed.

A smile crept across Tyler's face. "You're right. I'm not sorry at all."

"I think it's really sweet that you guys are still so physical after all this time." Chasity said, leaning forward to be heard.

"All this time?" Amanda asked. "You say it like we've been married for forty years."

"Sometimes it feels like it." Chris chuckled.

Amanda folded her arms. "I'll remember that when we get to the beach." She turned her head away and took in the surroundings. Thick forest stretched for miles in every direction. When she agreed to take a trip to Panama City, she thought they would be flying. They probably would have if Chris didn't buy a brand-new car. He was obsessed with this thing.

Chris threw the blinker on again and turned onto a small, two-lane road. A lopsided street sign proclaimed the road as "Martinville Highway."

Amanda glanced down at the GPS on her phone. A loading screen appeared, indicating the GPS was attempting to re-route them. "Um, babe. I think you took a wrong turn."

Chris shook his head. "Nah. I scouted this place out online. There is a charging station here. If we fully recharge now, we should be able to make it to the beach without any issues."

Through the windshield, the outskirts of a town peeked out from the trees. Old brick buildings, stained by years of neglect, lined the street. They cruised past the general store, a barbershop, and a run-down-looking gas station. Parked cars filled the available spots on either side of the road.

Chris slowed the car as he searched for the charging station. "Keep your eyes out for a place called Lowman Tires. Apparently, that's where we charge up."

"Guys." Tyler said from the back seat.

"What?" Chris asked, sounding a little irritated. He leaned forward in his seat, scanning the signs above the buildings.

Tyler spun around in his seat to look out the rear window. "Where are all the people?"

Amanda sat up straighter. Something seemed off about the town as soon as they pulled in, but she couldn't place it before.

There were no people. In a small town like this, on a weekday afternoon, she would expect to see people walking around the main street area. Her eyes drifted over to the general store. The lights were off. A plastic sign hung from the doorknob, signaling that the building was closed. She quickly shifted her eyes to the gas station. From this distance, it was hard to be sure, but she thought the pumps were shut off.

"It's just a small town, man." Chris said, dismissing his friend. "There's not a lot of people."

Chasity pointed to the right. "There's the tire shop!" Chris turned his wheel and started accelerating.

Seemingly out of nowhere, a group of kids emerged from a side alley on bicycles, peddling into the road in front of their car. Chris slammed on the brakes, causing the vehicle's tires to squeal in protest. Tyler lurched forward, smacking his forehead against the headrest.

"What the fuck?" Chris yelled. He threw his hands up, gesturing angrily at the kids.

Four of the boys continued their trek, riding right past the car as if nothing had happened. They went on to jump the opposite curb and disappear into another alley. A fifth boy lingered in front of the car. He sat atop his bike, both feet planted firmly on the ground and stared at Chris through the windshield.

"What's this kid's fucking problem?" He muttered. Lightly tapping the steering wheel, the car's horn let out a little squeak.

The kid didn't move. His chubby face remained emotionless, his pale skin sunburnt as if he had been outside for days.

"Move, kid!" Chris shouted, then slammed on his horn. The blaring horn cut through the serene town, disrupting its apparently peaceful existence.

After a few more minutes of staring each other down, Chris threw his car into park and opened his door. As soon as his shoe hit the pavement, the kid pushed off and rode after his friends. Chris lingered for a moment, then closed his door and put the car into drive.

"What was that about?" Chasity asked.

Tyler patted her leg. "There's nothing to do in towns like this." He shrugged his shoulders. "Little fucker is probably bored."

Calling the kid a "little fucker" solicited a slight chuckle from Chasity and Amanda. Chris still seemed perturbed by the whole situation as he aggressively slammed the car back into drive and pulled into the parking lot of Lowman's tires. The car eased over a black hose, ringing the bell inside the station. Chris stopped next to the charging port and got out of the vehicle. He shoved his door shut with enough force to rock the vehicle. Turning his attention to the charging station, he grunted in frustration. There were no working lights on the machine. Gritting his teeth, Chris smacked the side a few times.

"What's wrong?" Amanda asked.

Chris whirled around to see Amanda's head sticking out of the driver's window, her long brown hair falling messily around her.

"Fucking thing isn't working." Chris snapped. He marched past the driver's door.

"Where are you going?" Amanda called after him.

"Inside!" He shouted, while throwing his hands up dismissively. He strutted across the parking lot to the front door and pulled. The door didn't budge. He tried pushing it to no avail. "Come the fuck on." He whispered to himself. Cupping his fingers over his eyes, he pressed his face against the glass. Darkness engulfed the interior of the building. With the midday sun sitting high behind him, Chris could make out the outline of stacks of tires, a few chairs, and an old-timey cash register. He grunted and pushed off the door. He looked around at the empty streets around him. Old brick buildings surrounded the little tire shop, while a large park sat across the street. Chris continued scanning the area then froze.

A single kid was leaning against a tree in the park.

He was a tall, lanky boy. It was hard to tell from this distance, but Chris guessed his age to be about twelve. His head was shaved almost to the scalp and he wore a sleeveless t-shirt which showed off his sunburnt arms. The kid stared at Chris, not moving at all.

Raising a hand, Chris gave the kid a halfhearted wave.

Without reciprocating the wave, the kid rolled his back against the tree, disappearing behind it.

Chris shook his head. "This fucking town." He muttered. Goosebumps rolled up his arms. He scanned the streets again but saw nobody else. His gut begged him to get into the car and keep driving, but he knew they wouldn't make it to the next charging station. They had to recharge here.

He noticed the garage door of the shop was open, revealing what appeared to be an empty work area. Peering around the corner, he saw two hydraulic lifts, stacks of tires, and tools scattered about.

"Hello?" Chris yelled into the empty garage. Tentatively, he stepped through the open door. "Hey! I need to use your charging port!" He shouted.

No answer.

Chris was about to give up when he heard a noise from deeper within the garage. It was a metallic ping, as if someone had dropped a wrench or screwdriver. Stepping deeper into the garage, he yelled out again. "Come on, man. I just want a quick charge and then I'll be on my way."

No answer.

Fuck this. Chris thought to himself as he turned to leave. His heart skipped a beat and he cried out in surprise.

Standing between him and the car was the young boy from the park.

"Jesus Christ. You scared the shit out of me, kid." He laughed.

The kid crossed his arms, continuing to stare at Chris.

Waving his hand around the shop, Chris asked, "Hey, you wouldn't happen to know where the guy who runs this place is, would you?"

To his surprise, the kid nodded.

A smile stretched across Chris' face. "Where is he?" Chris asked hopefully.

The kid uncrossed his arms and pointed behind Chris.

Following the kid's gesture with his eyes, Chris slowly turned. His eyes stretched wide in surprise as he did.

The chubby kid who had blocked the road with his bicycle stood a few feet behind Chris, flanked on either side by a gang of other kids.

"What the..." Chris' words trailed off as he watched more kids emerge from behind the stacks of tires. Young boys, appearing to range in age from about six to fourteen, filled the garage, working their way toward Chris.

Chris put his hands up defensively and took a step away from the kids. "I, uh, I'm just going to go." He spun on his heels, coming face to face with the short-haired kid from the park.

There was a hard impact to his chest that forcefully expelled the air from his lungs. Slowly, he lowered his eyes to see the handle of a large kitchen knife protruding from his chest. Blood bubbled to the surface, carving a hot path down his torso. The shock of the moment faded away, allowing the agonizing pain in his chest to take over. A scream filled the air and for a moment, Chris thought it might have been his own, but it sounded far away. Looking up, he saw Amanda standing next to the Tesla, her hands over her mouth.

Chris' senses came flooding back to him all at once. Acting on pure instinct, he shoved the kid, putting all of his weight into the push. The kid toppled over, scraping against the concrete. A sickening crunch filled the air as the back of the boy's skull rebounded off the asphalt. Blood gushed from the kid's wound and puddled around his head.

Ignoring the injured child, Chris staggered forward. He willed his legs to move but they didn't seem to respond appropriately. He found himself falling forward more than walking. His feet seemed to jerk spastically, forcing him to stagger to the side.

Another crunch filled the air and intermingled with Amanda's screams. Feeling something smacking against his right leg, Chris lost his balance. He pitched hard to the right, crashing to the floor. His shoulder smashed into the ground with a deafening *pop*. A scream of agony left his lips. He knew he couldn't allow himself to linger. Rolling onto his stomach, careful not to drive the knife in further, he tried to pull his right leg underneath him. As soon as he moved his right leg, a blinding pain radiated throughout his body. Looking down, he saw a jagged shard of bone protruding through his jeans. He tried to scream but couldn't catch his breath. Pain tore through his body and darkness encroached on his vision. Rolling onto his back, he stared up at the afternoon sky.

Near the car, Amanda screamed and fought against Tyler's grip as he struggled to get her back into the car.

Chris stretched out his right hand, reaching for his wife. The coppery taste of blood filled his mouth as specks of blood erupted from his lips with each haggard breath.

The kids closed in around him, circling like hyenas around a kill. The chubby kid stood over him with a large wrench. He held it in one hand and repeatedly smacked it against the other hand, like a batter stepping up to the plate..

"You came to the wrong town, loser." The chubby boy said. His taunt was met with a chorus of laughter. One of the younger boys made the shape of an "L" on his forehead and danced, kicking his legs around wildly. Chubby kid smiled at the other children's taunts. He hoisted the heavy wrench above his head, his motion mimicked by the boys as they threw up their arms and cheered.

The chubby kid looked down at Chris, locking eyes with him. Chubby kid winked, then brought down the wrench with all his might.

The crack of metal against bone filled the air. Chris' skull gave way to the weight of the wrench. Blood spurted from an enormous crater in Chris' head. Lifting the wrench again, chubby kid watched Chris convulse on the ground. His legs twitched, his mouth opening and closing like a fish out of water.

"Should I hit him again?" The kid shouted.

A chorus of encouragement filled the air as the boys worked themselves into a blood-lust.

Amanda watched with tears streaming down her face as her husband vibrated on the floor and knew it was too late to save him. She allowed Tyler to push her back into the passenger seat. The children danced around wildly, several of them taking turns leaping over her dying husband. A young boy, Amanda judged to be about seven, rushed forward and plunged a screwdriver into Chris' stomach. She could do nothing but watch through the window as the boys laughed at the mess before them.

The chubby boy locked eyes with Amanda and smiled. He waved the blood-soaked wrench at her before bringing it down on Chris' head, causing the top half of his head to burst open like a dropped melon. His brains sprayed

out across the pavement, staining the sidewalk in gore.
Beside her, Tyler started up the car. She felt it lurch into
drive, the tires spinning momentarily before catching. The
car accelerated forward, jumping the curb and speeding
down the road. Amanda stared numbly into the passenger
mirror.

Chubby kid was swinging the wrench above his head,
raining down blood and chunks of brain matter on the
other kids. He threw the wrench into the road. He immediately barked commands at the other kids. Amanda
couldn't hear what the boy was saying, but she didn't need
to. He began frantically pointing toward their car. Several
boys appeared on bicycles, peddling hard in an attempt to
catch up to the car.

"They're coming." Amanda whispered.

In the back seat, Chasity leaned over and vomited onto
the floorboards. The sloshing of her puke splattering nearly forced Amanda to throw up as well. She swallowed the
hot bile pooling at the back of her throat.

"Jesus fucking Christ. What the fuck was that?" Tyler
screamed at the windshield. Turning the wheel abruptly,
the tires squealed. They sped down a random road, searching for a way out of town.

"The GPS." Amanda said flatly.

"What?" Tyler snapped. He took his eyes off the road to look at her, then immediately returned his gaze to the windshield.

"The GPS." She said again, pointing at the large screen in the middle of the dashboard.

Without answering, Tyler veered hard to the right, pulling the car to a stop between two red-bricked buildings. He quickly found the GPS app then froze. *Where should they go?* He racked his brain for the right answer. They could head back north, but that would likely take them back past the group of kids. Deciding to go south, he typed in Panama City, the route showing two hours left to drive. He had no intention of reaching their destination. As soon as they got out of this town, they would find a police station and get help.

"Should I call the police?" Chasity asked, wiping bits of her lunch off her chin.

"Yeah." Tyler said, throwing the car into reverse. He kicked himself for not thinking to call them sooner. "Yeah. Call them." He placed a hand on the headset of the passenger seat and turned around. Slamming on the gas pedal, the car accelerated backward.

Out of the corner of her eye, Amanda saw a flash of movement. She jerked her head toward the window and saw a trio of boys sprinting out from around one of the buildings. They threw something under the car and disappeared again.

Amanda opened her mouth to warn Tyler, but before she could, the concussive wave of an explosion rocked the car, smashing her head into the window. The rear of the car lifted off the ground, smashing back to the earth with a thud. Smoke swirled around the vehicle, obscuring the outside world.

Amanda's hand flew to her head, coming away slick with blood. She was faintly aware of someone in the vehicle screaming but couldn't comprehend the words.

Slowly, the world came back into focus. She spun around in her seat in time to see two boys attempting to drag Chasity out of the car. Little hands groped at her. They yanked on her blonde hair and pulled on her clothes. Chasity flailed around, scratching at her attackers.

Amanda heard a child cuss, then another yelled, "hit that bitch!" A hammer flew through the smoke, connecting with Chasity's head. The top of her skull crunched, giving way to the metal. Chasity went slack, slumping against the seat. A vacant expression came over her face. Another hand reached into the back seat. It grabbed Chasity's hair and jerked her head to the side.

Amanda watched the subtle rise and fall of Chasity's chest. The dazed woman's eyes fluttered. Amanda heard

Tyler's groans. He rubbed his head, struggling to fully regain consciousness. "Help her." Amanda croaked out.

"What?" Tyler mumbled.

Amanda grabbed her door handle and pushed the door open. "Help Chasity." She said with more force. Falling out of the car, Amanda rolled onto the ground. She fought to regain her composure. Taking in the scene around her, her mind struggled to piece together the chaos. The back tires of the car were shredded, the acrid smell of burnt rubber permeated the air. A small fire coated the asphalt under the car, the flames licking at the undercarriage. Smoke swirled around the car.

The sounds of Chasity screaming broke through the haze in her brain. Forcing herself to her feet, she staggered back toward the car. Through the windows, she watched Chasity get dragged out of the car. A trio of boys grabbed her by her hair and clothes. With several large heaves, they pulled her away from the vehicle and into the middle of the road.

The next few seconds came to Chasity in broken fragments, like a jigsaw puzzle that didn't fit together. Chasity's hands flew wildly, striking viciously at her attackers. The injured woman managed to rake her nails across one of their faces, drawing blood. The boy recoiled, grabbing his face and falling to his ass. He screamed out in pain.

"Kill her!" The injured boy screamed through his hands.

One of the other boys produced a box cutter. His thumb depressed the button, allowing the razor to slide out. Cocking his arm back, he took a swing at Chasity's face.

Chasity raised her arms in time to cover her face. The blade connected with her forearm. It cut deep, opening a massive gash and revealing the severed sinew of her muscle. She cried out in pain while desperately trying to squirm free of the kids. Her back scraped across the pavement as she wiggled backward, using her feet to drive her away from the boys.

Amanda willed herself to get up and help her friend. Taking several slow breaths, Amanda clambered to her feet. She took a single step when a loud whistle erupted from up the street.

Spinning around, Amanda saw an army of boys riding bicycles toward her. Chubby boy rode slowly behind them. He was still removing his fingers from his mouth when Amanda locked eyes on him. Smiling, he revealed yellowing teeth.

"Trey. Jerome. Take the old man out." He shouted. Two boys broke off from the convoy, veering their bikes toward the ruined Tesla.

Amanda's heart thundered against her chest. She took several steps away from the approaching boys. Unsure what to do, she watched as the smaller child pulled something black from his pocket.

In one swift motion, the boy jumped off his bike, his movement being matched by his companion. The two boys came together wordlessly. The first boy held up the black object while the other produced a lighter.

Amanda's mind flew back to the explosion that took out their car and she realized what was about to happen.

She spun on her heels and screamed. "Tyler! Get out of the car!"

When she looked back at the boys, the fuse was lit. It ignited in a flash of white light, sending sparks in all directions. It reminded Amanda of the sparklers Chris used to write her name in the air with every Fourth of July. As the kid approached, Amanda realized that was exactly what it was. A lone sparkler protruded from a tightly wrapped ball of electrical tape.

The boy sprinted across the open stretch of pavement between his bike and the car. He held up the homemade bomb like someone carrying the Olympic flame, displaying it proudly for his cheering comrades.

Inside the car, Tyler's blurry vision returned to normal. He fumbled with his seat belt, unable to release it. His eyes stretched wide as the boy approached.

Launching the improvised explosive device into the car, the boy dropped to his stomach and covered his ears. The bomb sailed through the air and landed in Tyler's lap.

Tyler's eyes shot up to Amanda, pleading with her for help. He grabbed the bomb, cocking his arm to throw it out of the car.

It exploded before he could throw it.

Amanda watched in horror as a fireball engulfed the vehicle. The concussive blast sent razor-like shards of glass in all directions. She felt the sting of hundreds of needles as they slammed into her. She allowed the impact to send her tumbling to the ground. Warm blood seeped up from the dozens of little cuts across her body. The pain was overwhelming. Every fiber of her body told her to just lay there. *What did she have to live for without Chris?*

The vision of Chris' massacred skull splayed out on the concrete flashed in her mind. Groaning in pain, she rolled to her side just in time to see several of the boys approaching. She frantically climbed to her hands and knees. Shattered glass tore into her palms and knees with every movement. She managed to crawl a few feet before the kids reached her.

Without warning, one of the boys ran up and kicked her in the ribs. Collapsing onto her back, she gasped for air and fought the urge to vomit at the same time. She stared up at a skinny black kid with a scar running down the side of his face. The boy dropped to his knees next to her and cocked his fist back.

"Wait!" Someone shouted. The boy looked back, fist still raised. Amanda lifted her head slightly to see chubby kid approaching. The kid lowered his fist, looking disappointed that he wasn't allowed to beat her to death.

"Let's take her back to the gym." Chubby boy nudged her with his foot. He pointed toward Chasity. "Bring her too."

The boy who had kicked her nodded. He pushed Amanda, forcing her to roll onto her stomach. Shards of broken glass filled her mouth, cutting her tongue and filling her mouth with blood. The boy jerked her hands above her head. She didn't resist as he slipped zip ties over her hands and clamped them down.

Another boy appeared at her side. Together, the boys grabbed her under her arms and hoisted her to her feet.

Amanda considered protesting but knew it was useless. These boys had already killed two people and she knew they weren't about to stop now. She tried to get her feet under her, but the pain in her legs with each step was blinding.

The boys dragged her past the car. She clenched her eyes shut, not wanting to see Tyler's ruined body. She was terrified at the thought of having the image of another dead friend seared into her memory.

They were nearly past the car when she heard a gasp.

"Amanda." A raspy voice pleaded.

She couldn't resist the urge. Opening her eyes, she saw Tyler.

Blood oozed from his ears and nose. His chest rose and fell in rapid succession. Amanda's eyes drifted over his tattered body. His right arm was missing below the elbow. Jagged shards of white bone protruded from the bloody stump. He held his left hand over his eviscerated stomach. Shriveled clumps of intestines peeked out through his fingers. The color had already drained from his face and his life was fading fast.

"Save." He sucked in a wet breath. "Her." He gasped. Specks of blood ejected from his lips, coating the charred steering wheel.

"I'll try." Amanda said as the boys dragged her away.

She saw an unconscious Chasity lying face down on the floor with her hands zip-tied behind her back.

The two boys released their grip on Amanda. She crumpled to the floor, her forehead bouncing off the asphalt. It should have hurt but numbness flooded her body as shock took over.

Amanda attempted to roll onto her side, only to see the bottom of a shoe coming at her face. She felt the impact for a split second, then darkness overtook her.

"Amanda." A voice hissed in the darkness. "Amanda, please wake up." The voice whispered again.

Amanda struggled to open her eyes. They seemed to be cemented together. Out of instinct, she tried to rub her face, only to realize she couldn't move her hands.

The flood of memories washed over her. Chris' skull cracked open on the ground. Tyler's ruined abdomen spilling his guts onto the floorboard of the car. Chastity being attacked by preteens. Chubby kid's smile. She jerked awake, forcing her eyes open.

She was on a makeshift stage in a large open room. Her eyes slowly adjusted to the dim lighting. A basketball hoop hung from the ceiling at the far end of the room. Looking around, she could make out bleachers lining the walls. They were in a gymnasium.

"Amanda." The voice said again.

Amanda jerked her head to the left. Chasity was restrained a few feet away, her zip tied hands secured above her head. Looking up, Amanda saw her own hands zip-tied to a hook. The tips of her fingers had turned purple and ached beyond belief.

"They're coming back soon, Amanda." Chasity whispered. "The fat kid told one of them to get a bat." Tears streamed from her eyes. "I don't want to die." Amanda saw the sobs building up in her friend's chest and prayed the girl wouldn't make much noise.

Amanda examined the hook above her head. It was a rusty shard of metal protruding from the concrete wall at her back. She pulled against the restraints. The metal hook wiggled slightly, showering her in concrete dust. She was about to pull again when the doors to the gymnasium flew open.

Chubby kid strutted into the room, followed by about twenty boys. If it wasn't for the blood coating their clothes, they would have looked like ordinary kids about to play a pickup game of basketball. In fact, one of the kids was holding a basketball. The kid dribbled twice, then pulled up and took a shot. The ball ricocheted off the backboard. Another kid rushed forward and grabbed the ball. "You're ass!" The kid jeered as he laid the ball up. It fell through the hoop with ease. The first kid flicked the other off.

"Enough." Chubby kid said. The kid with the ball dribbled a few more times, then rolled it across the floor, where it came to rest against the wall.

Chubby kid approached the stage and climbed onto it. His pudgy stomach jiggled as he struggled to get to his feet. He held out his hands at either side and waited for the rest of the kids to get into position.

"Do we want adults in our town?" He asked.

The crowd erupted into a fit of furious shouts and thrusting fists.

"We freed ourselves from our parents and their stupid rules!" He turned and pointed toward Chasity and Amanda. "They want there to be rules!"

"No rules!" A child shouted from the back of the crowd.

The chubby kid pivoted and pointed toward the crowd. "Who has the bat?" He asked.

A kid in the front row hoisted up an aluminum Louisville Slugger. Chubby kid grabbed it and thrust it into the air. In unison, the children cheered. He spun around with the bat, wielding it like an axe over his head. He brought it down quickly, stopping inches from Chasity's head. "Should I start with this one?" He asked.

A few of the children cheered, causing Chasity to break into hysterical sobs. "Please. Please. Please. You don't have to do this!" She pleaded. "We don't care about rules." She cried.

Chubby boy smiled. He swung the bat into his other hand, rubbing it against Amanda's cheek.

In that moment, Amanda resolved herself to her death and was determined not to give this little shit stain the satisfaction of forcing her to cry.

A few of the boys cheered. Chubby kid spun around. "I can't hear you!" He shouted. He pointed the bat at Amanda. "The brunette?" The crowd cheered louder this time. Chubby kid nodded and turned toward Chasity. "Or the blonde?"

The gymnasium erupted.

Chubby kid turned to face Chasity. She was shaking her head violently from side to side. Tears streamed down her face. She yanked against her restraints with all her might.

"Gotta give the people what they want." He said with a shrug.

Chubby kid pulled the bat to his shoulders and swung.

The metal bat crashed into Chasity's left knee, forcing the leg to give way, jutting backward. The crack of her bones was deafening. Chasity screamed as loud as she could. Chubby kid pulled the bat back again. He smiled as he swung it again, taking out her other knee. Just like before, the knee gave way. Chubby kid pulled back and swung, pulled back and swung. The baseball bat continued its savage dance, destroying different parts of Chasity's body with every strike.

Amanda closed her eyes, unable to bring herself to watch her best friend get beat to death. Eventually, Chasity's cries petered out until the chubby kid was panting and the smack of metal on skin was all that could be heard. Even the crowd had died down, their blood lust apparently satiated for now.

Amanda opened her eyes when the sounds of the bat impacting her friend stopped. She saw chubby kid standing next to Chasity, his face blood red with sweat pouring down his forehead. He glared at Amanda with hatred, then raised the bat one more time. With all of his might, he brought it down on Chasity's slumped head. The back of her skull caved into the shape of the bat, and Amanda knew her friend was dead.

Chubby kid wiped the sweat from his forehead, then pointed the bat at Amanda. "It's your turn." He said between pants. He walked across the stage, coming to a stop in front of her. Planting the bat onto the floor, the boy used it as a makeshift cane, allowing it to support his entire weight. He sucked in a deep breath. "I'm going to make yours fast." He whispered. "I'm too tired to do that again." He nodded toward Chasity's mangled corpse. Lifting the bat, he positioned it onto his shoulder and took another deep breath. He cocked his arms back to swing.

The door to the gymnasium burst open. A small blonde kid came rushing into the building.

"Robbie! There's another car coming!" The little kid shouted.

Chubby kid whirled around. He pointed into the crowd. "You know what to do!" He shouted.

Amanda watched as the sea of children's faces spun around and stormed out of the gymnasium. Chubby boy, who Amanda now knew was named Robbie, jumped off the stage and rushed off with the others. The door slammed shut behind him, leaving Amanda completely alone.

She lingered in silence, straining her ears for any hint of the boys. When she was confident the boys wouldn't come rushing back in, she stood up taller, creating a little slack in her restraints. Closing her eyes, she jumped, tucking her knees to her chest. The restraints around her wrist caught her full body weight, sending a wave of pain down her arms. The metal hook shook loose from the wall with a clunk. She collapsed to the ground, landing on her elbows.

Blood rushed back into her fingers. Needles of pain shot through her hands with each beat of her heart. She stayed on the ground for a moment, trying to gather her strength.

Amanda sucked in a deep breath and pushed herself to her knees. Slowly, she rose to her feet. Bolts of pain shot through her body with every movement. When she was once again upright, she looked around for a way to cut her bindings.

There was nothing except her dead friend behind her and the basketball in the corner. Giving up on cutting the bonds, she settled for the next best thing, escape. Leaping from the stage, she jogged across the basketball court to the door.

She grabbed the handle and turned it. Pushing the door open inch by inch, she peered through the crack.

One of the boys was standing a few feet away with his back toward her. He was staring toward the direction of the highway.

Amanda closed her eyes and took a deep breath. When she opened her eyes, she saw red. Her pulse quickened and her restrained hands balled into fists. She threw the door open and sprinted toward the boy.

She slipped her arms over his head before he could turn around. The zip-ties landed just under his chin. Throwing herself backward, Amanda yanked the kid down on top of her. She squeezed as hard as she could. The zip-ties dug deep into the boy's skin, drawing thin rivulets of blood. The boy thrashed wildly, groping manically at the restraint around his neck. Blood from his tearing skin fell from the kid, decorating Amanda's face in a macabre war paint. The sensation of his warm blood only made her pull harder.

Slowly, the kid stopped thrashing. He lazily slapped at her hands a few times before going slack. Amanda kept pulling, determined to put the murderous little bastard down for good. After a few more minutes, she released her hold on the boy and slipped her hands back over his head. She shoved him off of her and stood up, gasping for breath.

Knowing the other boys could come back at any minute, Amanda bent over and worked her hand into the boy's pocket. Her fingers danced over something metal. She fought with the object for a few seconds until she grasped it and pulled it from the pocket. Her heart soared.

It was a box cutter.

Extending the blade, she flipped the cutter around in her hands and sliced through the zip-ties with ease. Flexing her fingers, she wiggled them around, forcing blood into her hands. Tossing the box cutter in her pocket, she patted the kid down. Something bulged in his other pocket. Pulling it out, she smiled.

It was one of the homemade bombs and a lighter.

Voices approached from around the corner of the building. Not waiting to see who it was, Amanda turned and ran in the opposite direction. She dipped around a corner just as the boys came into view.

Robbie was leading the group, his shirt lifted to reveal his tubby, pale stomach. The boys behind him were covered in even more blood, evidence of another kill.

"Dude, his head exploded!" One of the boys shouted as several of the boys laughed.

Their laughs were cut short by Robbie's shouts. He dropped to the floor, pressing his hands against the dead boy's chest. "Mikey's fucking dead!" Robbie shouted. He leaned against the wall, using it to help himself to his feet. He rushed across the sidewalk and threw the gymnasium door open. A few seconds later, he exploded through the door, crashing into the crowd of kids. Trying to avoid the bigger kid's ire, several of the kids fell down.

"She got away!" Robbie shouted. His head jerked wildly from side to side, searching for Amanda. "Spread out and find her!" He shouted. Like ants, the boys scattered in all directions.

Amanda peeked around the corner to see three boys running in her direction. She locked eyes with one of the kids, his face morphing into a look of surprise.

"She's over here!" He shouted.

Amanda looked down at the explosive in her hand. Dipping back behind the wall, she sparked the lighter and held it against the one exposed sparkler. It burst into flames, casting a blinding white light. She dropped the explosive at her feet and ran.

She pumped her arms and legs as fast as they would carry her. Amanda couldn't remember the last time she had run, but her screaming hamstrings told her it had been a long time. Her lungs burned with each deep breath as she sprinted across an empty field.

"There she..." The boy's proclamation was cut short by the explosion.

Amanda swirled around to see two of the kids lying face down on their stomachs, unmoving. The third kid was on his back with the bloody stump of what used to be his right leg sticking up in the air. It took a moment before he started screaming, but when he did, the anguish in his shouts was heartbreaking. As much as she wanted to kill these little bastards for murdering her friends, they were still children. Her own sense of morality tugged at her.

She took a half-step toward the injured boy, contemplating helping the kid when Robbie rounded the corner. The look of pure hatred on his face washed away any remaining sympathy Amanda might have had for those monsters.

Without waiting for the others, Robbie took off, running across the field toward Amanda. She watched him run. It was an embarrassingly slow pace, his stomach bouncing around as he did. The boy only slowed with each step as his breathing grew deeper. Behind him, the other boys emerged from around the corner to be greeted with the carnage of their three dead or dying friends. They all froze there, eyes bouncing from the bodies on the ground, to Robbie struggling to run across the field, and back to the bodies. It was as if they were unsure what they should do next.

Amanda wondered if the boys had bit off more than they could chew, only just now realizing this wasn't a game. She waited for Robbie to approach, no longer afraid of the chubby little shit. Slipping her hand into her pocket, she withdrew the box cutter and extended the blade.

Robbie slowed as he approached, fists up. "I'm going to…" He trailed off, trying to catch his breath. "Beat you to death." He gasped. He stepped forward and took a swing.

Amanda sidestepped the lazy punch and thrust the blade toward Robbie's face. It caught him at the corner of his lip, slicing through his cheek like butter. The skin spread apart to reveal his teeth and tongue. Robbie shrieked and grabbed his face. She swung again. This time, the blade ran across the boy's chest, spilling blood down his shirt.

"No!" He begged.

Amanda swung again and again. Opening new wounds with every swipe.

Robbie collapsed to the ground, hands up. Amanda fell upon him like a lion on its prey. With a barbaric howl, Amanda drove the blade into Robbie's throat, slicing until she met bone. She yanked on the box cutter, desperately trying to decapitate her husband's killer.

Utterly exhausted, she pushed herself off the dying boy, standing over him as blood gushed from his severed neck. He held her gaze even as he coughed up blood. Never once did the hatred in his eyes falter. Amanda couldn't help but wonder what had happened to make him this way. She knew it didn't matter now, but the thought nagged at her. They stayed like that, tangled in a battle of wills, until the light faded from Robbie's eyes.

When Amanda finally tore her eyes from the dead boy, she saw his army of kids slowly backing away. Terrified expressions looked around, frantically seeking a place to go. Without hesitation, she marched across the field toward them, the bloody box cutter still dangling from her fingers.

The shocked expressions on the kids' faces became clearer as she approached. She held up the box cutter, menacingly displaying it in front of her. "Are you all done now?" She screamed.

Several of the kids started crying, backing away even further. When none of the kids stepped up, she spoke again. "Good."

Amanda continued walking through the crowd of boys. They parted like the Red Sea, allowing her to pass through. Amanda continued walking south until she hit the highway. She continued walking through the night without stopping, eventually reaching another town. Ignoring the strange looks, she walked through the downtown streets and into the police station.

Still covered in blood, she explained the events to a very old and very surprised detective.

When she was done, the detective leaned back, steepling his hands in front of his face. He sat like that for a long time. Eventually, he dropped his hands.

"What happened to the rest of the kids?" He asked.

Amanda shook her head. "Man, fuck them kids."

About the
Author

Timothy King is an adult horror author who enjoys delving into the complexities of human nature. When he is not writing spine-chilling tales, he is spending time with his wife and kids in beautiful Tampa, Florida.

You can find him on Facebook, Tiktok or by emailing him at:

Timothykingauthor@gmail.com

If you enjoyed this book, please consider leaving a review on Amazon or Goodreads!

Made in United States
Cleveland, OH
05 September 2025

20169378R00163